A Beth-Hill Novel:
The Shadows Trilogy, Book 3:
Bound In Shadows

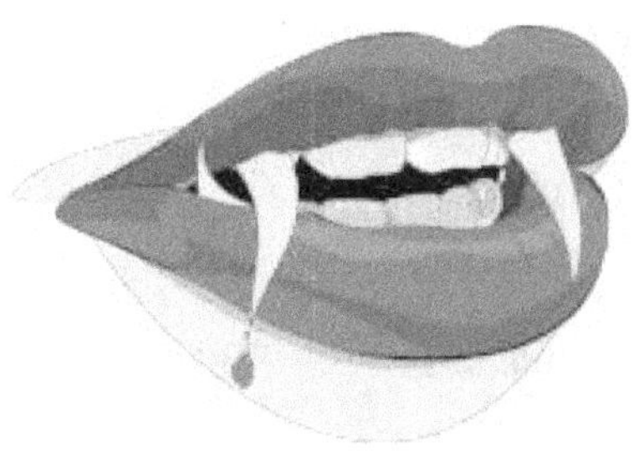

By Jennifer St. Clair

Writers Exchange E-Publishing

http://www.writers-exchange.com

A Beth-Hill Novel: The Shadows Trilogy, Book 3: Bound in Shadows

Copyright 2015, 2023 Jennifer St. Clair

Writers Exchange E-Publishing

PO Box 372

ATHERTON QLD 4883

Cover Art by: Jatin and Sandy Cummins

Published by Writers Exchange E-Publishing

http://www.writers-exchange.com

To Jenna

Chapter 1

Nicodemus opened his eyes. For a moment he could not remember why he stared out from a strange mirror at such terrible destruction; then memories started to trickle forth into his mind. Skade. Espen. Michael. Terrin escaping.

Dying.

He touched his chest and saw his body, lying forlorn and forgotten in the midst of debris. They had left it behind, of course--the survivors were more important--but he still felt a bit lost that they had left *him* behind. How would he go to his Queen, when he did not know where Espen lived?

He thought he might be able to follow the portal, if Skade had not set barriers that kept him trapped in this mirror. He doubted she'd had time to form anything in the way of a cage; Terrin's spell had eaten her strength even as she saved his life one more time.

Of course, she could be dead already, and perhaps Espen would never return for him. Perhaps he would haunt Leysan's halls forever, or until Teluride returned as its King.

If Teluride returned.

A movement near the door caught his eye, and Nicodemus watched as a dark lump on the floor crawled into the light of a dying torch.

Evidently he wasn't the only survivor.

At first, Nicodemus didn't recognize Terrin's partner, for Cathan's face was streaked with soot and blood, and the look in his eyes was far from sane. But when he realized Nicodemus watched him from the mirror, the look in his eyes chilled what was left of the Ghost's soul.

Cathan spat blood on the ground and pushed himself to his knees. "They left you behind as well, I see."

"I would prefer to be left behind if my Queen's life is saved in my stead," Nicodemus whispered warily.

"If Terrin infected her with his spell, she's as good as dead," Cathan replied, and saw Nicodemus' body lying five feet in front of him.

A strange look passed over his face at the sight. Nicodemus tensed, waiting for him to do something unspeakable, but Cathan merely stared.

"She will not die," Nicodemus whispered, refusing to court the thought.

Cathan laughed. "Everyone dies."

Without bothering to ask permission, he set about undressing Nicodemus' body until it lay naked and bare on the rubble-strewn floor.

"What are you doing?" Nicodemus asked. Cathan didn't bother to reply, and in a moment, when his exposed skin started to shimmer, Nicodemus realized what he planned to do. "No!"

Cathan smiled and stared at his new reflection in the mirror. "What will happen to you if I break that mirror?"

Nicodemus couldn't tear his eyes away from Cathan's new face. "I...I don't know." If he knew where Espen lived, he'd try to go there now, to warn her, to...

Cathan's fist lashed out, but the mirror didn't break. Nicodemus cringed away from him, entranced despite himself. Had his face ever shown such hate? He braced himself for another blow, but Cathan paused.

"Wait. I might need you, if this works." He patted down his pockets, cursed, then disappeared into the hallway, limping slowly past Nicodemus' body. A moment later, he was back with a crystal pendant swinging from one clenched fist. "I should be happy he had a spare."

"A...a spare?" The sight of Cathan's face cast a strange sense of deja vu over Nicodemus' mind. Had this happened before?

And then he remembered. Cathan had worn Michael's face in Iomar to steal him from Skade, and now...now he wore...

Cathan knelt beside Nicodemus' body and sliced one flaccid arm with a small dagger. Sluggish blood seeped out--blood that shouldn't have seeped anywhere if he were truly dead.

Nicodemus couldn't breathe. He watched as Cathan smeared blood on the crystal pendant and his free hand, then struggled to his feet. He watched as Cathan approached the mirror to place a bloody handprint on the glass.

As before, Nicodemus felt himself drawn to the crystal, but that was not the only source of blood in the room.

He had split himself in two before, in essence, to keep an eye on two things at once. He drew upon that skill to save himself now, and pushed as much of his...spirit...into his body as the crystal drew the rest of his spirit into its prison.

Coldness chilled his soul. Blackness threatened to suck away what little life remained in his body, but he held right to consciousness and felt his wounded heart begin to beat.

He watched through slitted eyes as Cathan stowed the crystal away, and felt the velvet folds of a familiar bag close over part of his sight. The larger part remained, but living eyes were no match for ghostly ones. He did not know how long he could stay in his body...or how long he had to live with Terrin's spell eating away at his very limited strength.

He only knew he had to try to warn Espen and his Queen that Cathan now wore his face...before it was too late.

Chapter 2

Rumors had always flowed quickly through the Seven Kingdoms. Each King and Queen--or Steward in Aberdus' case--had heard of the death of King Valdis, and Terrin's ascension to the throne before a month had passed. Loathe to involve themselves in what seemed to be a minor struggle for the throne, they kept their minds on their own affairs, but listened avidly for any news. By the time Skade vanished from her bedroom, Cynara, Severin's Queen, had already set in motion her limited supply of spies, but she found no new information, and the Kingdom of Iomar had no statement for the rest of Cruinne.

Although she had promised Kyne she wouldn't send her out again, Cynara doubted she had any other choice. Kyne was, after all, already intimately acquainted with the inside of Leysan's walls. She knew Terrin as well, and his son, both of whom seemed to have vanished with Skade. She knew how to keep to the shadows and move around unseen. That had not helped her last time--Cynara had yet to discover what foul tortures Kyne had endured at Terrin's hands--but as far as she had been able to discern, Terrin had vanished from Leysan some days before.

It only took her fifteen minutes to find her sister. Kyne was, after all, predictable in her hiding places.

"I know why you've come."

Cynara could barely see the dark figure of her sister nestled in between two gargoyles at the top of the west wall of the castle. "If you know why I've come, then I know your answer," she replied.

Kyne shifted on her perch. "I've heard...disturbing news."

"As have I," Cynara said. "The Queen of Iomar has vanished."

"Her son is said to be involved," Kyne said.

Cynara frowned. "I hadn't heard that piece. Do you have spies where I do not?"

Kyne slid from her perch and leapt lightly to the stairs. She stared down at her sister for a moment, then smiled. "Of course I do, sister dear. But my spies know no more than you now. We are equal in that respect."

"How did you know of her son, then?" Cynara tried to remember if she had ever met Skade's son, but she had only met the Iomarian *Queen* once or twice. She couldn't remember a son at all. But then again, Iomar was the least social of the Seven Kingdoms and did not usually involve itself in mainland affairs.

"He was exiled ten years ago," Kyne said. "He had something to do with a scandal Skade covered up."

"A scandal? What kind of scandal?" Cynara asked.

Kyne shrugged and sat down on one of the lower steps. "I haven't been able to discover anything else but that. Whatever the secret is, it's buried deep. No one in Iomar will talk."

Cynara tucked this interesting information away in the back of her mind for later, and focused on the task at hand. "I need you to go to Leysan," she said.

Kyne just stared at her.

"Please, Kyne. I'm not asking you as a Queen. I'm asking you as a sister."

"That's worse," Kyne said sourly. "I'd almost rather you ask as my Queen."

"What you told me..." she sighed, "I have a feeling that whatever Terrin plans will destroy the Seven Kingdoms. It might take years, but I..."

"You don't think he will stop at his brother's throne?" Kyne asked.

"If he has taken Skade, then, no, I don't," Cynara said. "And if he has taken Skade, he has overpowered the most powerful Queen in Cruinne."

Kyne nodded. "And that would mean he can overpower anyone."

"Yes." Cynara didn't want to worry about Terrin and his plans, but she couldn't help herself. Severin's borders had been quiet for too many years to count. They still maintained an army, but not one of the soldiers had seen a battle fiercer than the occasional skirmish with the bandits who preyed on travelers through the mountains.

And she had met Teluride once; a long time ago when he was young and his mother still lived. No one deserved to be blamed for a murder unless they were truly guilty. And she could not believe he was guilty.

"I should refuse," Kyne said slowly. "You did swear to me you wouldn't ask me to go back."

"I know I did." Cynara would have wrung her hands if she thought it would help. "But..."

Kyne sighed. "Yes, I know. I'll admit that I've been curious to see what has happened. I left Alban and the prince and the vampire in Skade's care, but if she is gone..."

"Then where are they?" Cynara whispered.

"Exactly." Kyne hesitated. "I will go to Leysan. And I will try to contact Iomar as well. They know me there, at least. And I will send word."

"Thank you," Cynara said. "As both your Queen and your sister...thank you."

Kyne's smile did not reach her eyes. "Thank me when I return," she said. "For if you're right, and Terrin does not mean to stop with his brother's throne, I might not return. But I will send word. I promise you that."

She left at dawn the next morning, heading down the mountain to Leysan...and hopefully, answers.

Chapter 3

In the end, Espen almost had to pry Michael's fingers from his mother's arm. Only Enapay's voice shocked him out of numbness and brought him crashing back to the present.

"Daddy!"

Michael threw his arms around his daughter and held her close. He breathed in the scent of her, that unique smell children have, and tried to shut out what had happened in one desperate moment before sanity prevailed.

He opened his eyes and raised his head. "Espen?"

"She's alive," Espen said from where she stood over Skade's motionless body.

Considering the amount of magic her last two spells had cost, Michael knew she should be dead. More powerful people than the Queen of Iomar had died after doing less.

He did not want to ask the next most obvious question for fear of Espen's reply. But he could not live without knowing, either. Even if Espen sent him back, he could not return home without knowing if she would live. "Will she..."

"Questions later, Michael," Espen said. "Let me stabilize your mother's condition before I make any assumptions. Okay?"

Michael nodded. "I'll...I'll just stay here." For the first time since he stepped through Skade's portal, he took time to look around.

He had been in Espen's house once before, a long, long time ago. It hadn't changed much since then. The amount of clutter had grown, which did not surprise him, but the basic layout of the house remained the same.

He remembered a time when the house and Espen's source of power had worked against him, and shivered as long-buried memories raised their ugly heads.

He had to remind himself that he had not been accused of any crime this time. That he had not been in prison, but had been dragged into this unwillingly. But even with that assurance, it was hard not to feel on edge. He had only spent eight of the last twenty-eight years free, after all. And liberty was still enough of a novelty for the possibility of imprisonment to be all the more undesirable.

Enapay fell asleep in his arms an hour after Michael stepped through the mirror. He sat against the wall, cradling her against his chest, too unsure of his place to demand a bed for his daughter or an explanation from anyone.

The witch worked on his mother silently, with only the barest illumination of healing power to light her way.

Michael could have told her that her power would not work on Terrin's spell. He had tried to heal some of the earlier victims with his own paltry healing talent, with disastrous results. But since Skade didn't seem to be getting any worse, he supposed Espen knew what she was doing. After all, she *was* the head of the Healer network, and he was only an exiled prince.

After a little while, even though he did not want to fall asleep, he found it easier to close his eyes and lean his head back against the wall. Even though his wounds were nothing compared to what Terrin had done to Skade, he could not ignore how they sapped his strength. He had tried so hard to do the right thing. To redeem himself in his mother's eyes. Even though he had made a life for himself in exile, he always held that hope that someday his mother would forgive him and welcome him home.

Now he would never know.

"Michael?"

Michael awoke with a start. He opened his eyes to find Enapay still asleep in his arms, and Espen standing in front of him, her expression a strange mixture between concern and amusement.

"Where are you hurt?" Espen asked as soon as she was certain she had his attention.

Michael ignored her question. "Is my mother..."

"She's stable, for now, and sleeping comfortably in another room," Espen said. "I'll let you see her when she wakes up. Now answer my question."

"I'm fine."

Espen stared at him. "Martyring yourself isn't the right way to go about regaining her trust, Michael," she finally said. "You're as bad of a liar as your mother. Now, tell me where you're hurt and I'll let you meet the others."

The others. Michael smoothed down Enapay's hair. "The others?" He had seen Zaira through his makeshift mirror, but who else... And then he remembered Terrin's odd accusation. "His son? You have his son?"

"I have both his sons," Espen said. "Alban and Alexander."

Michael shook his head. "I had nothing to do with..."

"I'm not saying you did," Espen said. "I'm just trying to bring you up to date."

Michael sighed. "I'm not sure I *want* to be brought up to date. I'd made my peace, Espen. I..."

"The eighty-five people your mother's spells hold in stasis haven't made their peace with you," Espen said, an undercurrent of anger running through her voice. "We've searched for a cure for ten years now, Michael. How much longer will we have to look?"

Michael's cheeks burned at the grisly reminder of what he had allowed to happen. He could not believe how naive he had been, trusting Cathan, Nicodemus, and Terrin with no thought of what they intended to do with their creation. He should have been the responsible one, but instead he had ignored common sense and embraced ruin.

He had been so happy, in exile, when he found a place he could let down his guard, and look what had happened then.

"I didn't know you were able to save anyone," he finally whispered, not daring to glance up at Espen's face.

"There's a lot you don't know," Espen said. "And I'll try my best to bring you up to date. But first..."

Michael raised his head. "Wait."

Espen frowned at him. "Michael."

"No." Michael struggled to stand with Enapay in his arms. "I'm not badly hurt, honest. I just...what happened to Nicodemus?"

"That's a very good question," Espen said. "And the short answer is, I don't know. Skade *did* manage to put him back into the mirror, I think, but I have no idea where he went from there."

"He's gone?" Michael struggled with vague memories. "Terrin...Terrin escaped through a portal."

"I know." Espen knelt beside him and held out her arms. "Let me put Enapay in one of my spare rooms."

Michael shook his head, unwilling to release her just yet. "I almost lost her."

"But you didn't," Espen said. "She's here, with you."

This was true, but Michael still did not want to give her up. "Terrin escaped through the portal my mother created. The portal to your house."

"Yes. But he changed its destination. If he hadn't, he'd be in custody right now."

Michael closed his eyes. A moment later, he felt Espen carefully pry his daughter from his grasp. He thought to protest, but he couldn't seem to gather up enough strength to open his eyes.

"Michael." Her voice lacked all anger, and he remembered that Healers were bound to help anyone who came to them for aid. "Where are you wounded?"

Michael finally pried open his eyes. "I'm not..." he sighed, "I hit my head. And I think...I think Cathan..."

Espen gently lifted up his bloody shirt. A moment later, Michel felt the first stirring of healing magic course through his veins. It wasn't an entirely pleasant feeling, but he did not have enough strength to complain.

"You're lucky you didn't faint from loss of blood," Espen remarked after the bloody wound in his side had healed under her touch. "Anywhere else?" She touched his knee.

Michael stayed her hand. "That's an old wound."

"I know. But it's not properly healed, even though I feel the work of another Healer here," Espen said. "It shouldn't bother you at all."

"It...it reminds me," Michael whispered, almost too weary to care what she discovered about his life in exile.

"Reminds you of what?" Espen asked.

"My other mistake." He would go no further with this line of questioning. She did not need to know how his life had turned out while in exile; only that he was not the person he had once been. But he couldn't seem to keep his mouth shut. "I've...I've only been free for eight years."

"You've been gone for ten years here," Espen reminded him.

"Twenty-eight years where I ended up," Michael whispered. Even with Espen's healing, he desperately needed to sleep. "And I spent twenty of those years in Hell."

Espen's hands stilled on his knee. "Ah."

Michael managed to crack open his eyes far enough to see the neutral expression on her face. "Ah?"

"Sennet told me about you," Espen said, naming the Healer who had healed the original damage to his knee. "I didn't put two and two together until now."

Since Espen was the Head of the Healer network, Michael was surprised to hear she hadn't put two and two together sooner. After all, how many *other* exiled princes were there who ended up in Hell? He half-expected her to order him out of her house, but she did not.

"You need to rest," she finally said. "I can heal your wounds, but I cannot replenish your strength."

"I know," Michael said. Sennet had said the same thing. "I'll rest." He allowed Espen to help him up. His knee twinged in protest after being in one position for so long, but it held.

"I've put you in a room right beside Enapay's," Espen said. "You'll be able to hear her if she needs you; I promise you that."

"Thank you," Michael said, and meant it.

Espen fixed him with an unreadable stare. "Help us fix this, and you'll get much more than thanks."

That thought stayed with him even after darkness bore him away, coloring his dreams with the faint hope of redemption.

Chapter 4

"Zaira escaped, didn't she?" It had only taken a little power to change Skade's portal to deposit Terrin in Glinyeu, but it had taken him the better part of an hour to track down its mad king.

Eabon's eyes were red and crusted, his mouth ringed with weeping sores. "She's gone."

"Dead?"

Eabon shrugged, as if his daughter's death truly meant nothing.

"Did you kill her?" Terrin demanded, too weak to back his words with power. His wounds had stopped bleeding, at least, but the shards of Skade's beads still dug into his skin. It would take more power than he currently possessed to remove all traces of the cursed Queen from his body, and he knew of only one way to regain that much power, since Alban had also been lost to him.

"Did you kill her, Eabon?"

Eabon's hand twitched. "She...she..."

"What did she tell you?" Perhaps his Dreamer had disclosed some pertinent piece of information that would help him get rid of Skade and her network of allies once and for all.

"She..."

Terrin sighed. "It would be unwise to try my patience, Eabon."

"She said she saw my death." Eabon's eyes flashed when he raised his head. "She said you intended to kill me. Is this true?"

For a moment, Terrin didn't know what to say. He stared at the old King, remembering how he had been before Zaira's 'death', before the creation of the spell that had nearly been the death of so many people. The Eabon of old had been a worthy partner. This Eabon...this Eabon was not.

"Yes, it's true," Terrin said. "I do intend to kill you." He saw no reason to lie.

Eabon opened his mouth, and then closed it; evidently shocked Terrin had been so forthcoming.

"I didn't kill your Dreamer," Eabon said, as if that declaration of innocence would save him.

Terrin smiled. "That's good to know, but I'm still going to kill you."

There was no pleasure in killing a mad, old man, and even less in prolonging what had to be done. Years ago, to plan for this very possibility, Terrin had crafted a spell that he called into being now, even though it took most of the rest of his strength.

Eabon gasped and choked, his face rapidly purpling as Terrin's spell cut off all flow of air to his lungs. It did not take him long to expire, and Terrin drank the dying remnants of what power he had possessed, a taste sweeter than the finest wine.

Eabon's paltry powers would not give him much strength, but it would be enough to cast the shards of Skade's beads from his body before she realized how badly she could hurt him.

Even with both sons gone and his plans in disarray, he had to believe this was merely a setback and not the end.

After all, he had infected Skade with his spell, and even the vast network of healers that claimed Espen as its head had not been able to find a cure.

Chapter 5

It took Kyne less than three days to reach Leysan's borders, and a day after that to reach the castle. As night fell, she rode up to the gates, only to find them open and bare of guards.

This did not bode well. No sane king would leave his castle unguarded. But could she truly call Terrin sane?

Her relief at returning home to Severin had been short-lived. Truly, no one had blamed her for leaving Iomar; her duty was finished and she had other orders to fulfill. But leaving Alban, the vampire, and Teluride with Skade had seemed a good idea at the time. Now, with Skade missing, she doubted her prior wisdom. Would things have worked out differently if she had taken them back to Severin? Or would *Cynara* be missing, as Skade was, no doubt to Terrin's treachery?

She rode inside with her sword unsheathed, but met no one in the courtyard. Indeed, the entire castle seemed to be deserted, as if every living thing had fled from Terrin's power.

She entered the hall to silence marred only by the fluttering of bats overhead. The first thing she saw inside the cavernous room was the mirror that had hung over the fireplace--now broken beyond repair.

Thin threads of some awesome spell hung in the air at intervals, as if some great battle had been fought throughout the entire castle. Kyne eyed them dubiously, but they were dead and withered. The unknown wizard could call them to life, though, so she cut down the ones she could reach and hoped she would be forewarned if the remaining threads began to grow.

An hour after she entered the castle, she crept up the winding staircase. Almost at once, she smelled the unmistakable stench of death.

It took her only fifteen minutes more to find the King's Council.

By the look of things, they had been dead for weeks. Flies and maggots feasted on what was left of their flesh, and by their twisted skeletons, she surmised they had died by deceit more than magic. Shattered crystal goblets on the floor and table gave mute testimony to their deaths.

But why kill the Council? They could have strengthened Terrin's claim to the throne. To blatantly murder a group of defenseless men...Kyne could not imagine the depths of Terrin's madness. And as she moved through the castle, her unease only grew.

A sense of something...different drew her down the stairs again and into the dungeons, where she hoped not to find the bodies of those she'd left behind. But what she found, in a cell overrun with rats and covered with rotting straw, left her more puzzled than relieved at the lack of bodies.

A single red bead, glowing in the muck on the floor, strangely unmarked by the filth around it. Kyne knew of only one person who wore such beads. Did that mean the Queen of Iomar had once been a prisoner here? If so, where was she now?

A scrap of dark cloth caught on the edge of a large hole in the wall caught her eye. Kyne tucked the bead in her pocket and carefully made her way to the other side of the cell. The long strip of cloth was not instantly familiar, but when she realized where she'd seen such cloth before, she knew something had gone horribly wrong in Iomar.

It was a scrap of Iomarian cloth, intricately embroidered along the edge. The bottom hem of a shirt, and kin to a shirt she had last seen the vampire wearing. Did that mean the *vampire* had been prisoner here? And if that were so, where was *he* now?

She fixed her gaze on the hole. It was too small for her to fit inside, but small enough for the vampire's thin form. He could have found a way out of the castle through some forgotten causeway, she supposed, but she knew she could not count on that.

If the vampire had been prisoner here, then where was Alban? And what had happened to Teluride, the rightful King of Leysan? Was he dead, a victim of his Uncle's bid for the throne?

Kyne crouched down near the hole and reached through it until her arm encountered another wall. The space between the walls seemed to be wide enough for her to fit through, but did she truly want to explore deeper into the castle, not knowing what she might find? Or should she try to find an unbroken mirror and contact Iomar? If she confronted them with proof that something had gone terribly wrong, would they admit to her that their Queen had vanished? She had a feeling that she wouldn't find any usable mirrors in Leysan. Terrin, or someone, seemed to have broken them all.

So that left the hole. If the vampire had been in this cell and had crawled through the hole, then Kyne had to make sure he wasn't lying wounded wherever it ended. If she discovered later that she had left him to die in Leysan's dungeons, she would never be able to forgive herself.

It took her an hour to work more stones loose from the hole and make it big enough for her to squeeze through. She left no sign of her passage behind as the vampire had, and found the resulting passageway just large enough for her to crawl through. She was just about to venture down into the murky darkness when she heard a sound above her in the castle.

Above? How could she hear something in the castle proper through *feet* of stone?

A footstep; not just a sound. Kyne's dagger was in her hand even before she realized she had been followed.

But who could have followed her? A peasant? Had Terrin left a guard?

She had not explored all the upper floors of the castle, not after seeing the rotting bodies of the Council. She'd assumed the castle to be empty.

She had *assumed.* The last time she'd assumed something, Alban had caught her in a spell.

And what if they stole her horse?

On silent feet, Kyne slipped out of the dungeon cell and crept up the stairs. The footsteps continued until she opened the door, and then even the echoes had faded away by the time she stepped out into the main hall.

Had the footsteps gone upstairs? What would happen if a peasant discovered the bodies of the Council? Someone would raise an alarm and the castle would be bombarded.

Not that rioting would be such a bad thing, Kyne thought. That would get some of the other kingdoms involved, and Terrin would have a difficult time keeping hold of Leysan's throne.

Of course, that might make it more difficult for Teluride to regain his throne, but Kyne was not at all certain he would be capable of ruling an entire kingdom without a memory.

On the off chance the footsteps *had* gone upstairs, she ascended to the second floor of the castle again.

No one had disturbed the Council's bodies. As she closed the door behind her, she noticed a faint light in one of the rooms a few doors down.

Cautiously, she crept down the hall, her sword out and ready for any sign of attack.

Although there was a torch, the room seemed to be empty. Debris lay strewn around the room, but a large mirror had escaped most of the destruction. A smear of what looked like blood stained the surface of the glass. Debris littered the room; wooden casings from the blown out windows and shattered furniture covered the floor. Glass glittered in the light of the torch, as well as multicolored shards of what looked like...beads?

At least the mirror was whole. Kyne could contact Cynara and let her know what she had found so far. Or, what she had *not* found.

She stepped into the room, fairly confident that it was empty. But she didn't notice the narrow doorway of a closet until she was halfway to the mirror. She hesitated, remembering the footsteps. She had no proof that someone had walked into this room, of course. But it wouldn't hurt to check.

She took the torch from the wall and stepped up to the broken door. A small bed was the first thing that caught her eye. She didn't notice the body lying on the floor beside it until she stepped on one bloodstained hand and heard a faint moan.

She did not draw her sword. The sole survivor, unless she counted the footsteps, was in no shape to attack anyone. Kyne stuck the torch in a nearby sconce, but it shed only enough light for her to tell that the young man was naked. He had pulled a threadbare blanket from the bed to cover his body, but that seemed to be the extent of his strength.

Kyne rolled him over and stared down at a vaguely familiar face. Bloodstained blond hair stuck out from his head at odd angles and deep purple shadows circled his closed eyes. His skin was milky pale, as if he had been indoors for a long time.

The wound in his chest had caused much of the blood, but Kyne didn't think it looked life-threatening, at least not yet. In fact, it seemed to have healed somewhat already, even though she knew he couldn't have been lying unconscious for as long as the Council had been rotting in the other room. He would have died from starvation, or thirst, or something else by now.

His fingers were long and knobby, and without the calluses that would define him as a peasant or someone who worked with his hands. Sparkling bits of colored glass were embedded in the palm of one hand, as if he had taken a handful of the glittering shards and ground them into his skin. But why would he want to do that?

And who was he? That nagging familiarity would not leave her alone. Kyne unwrapped him from his cocoon to make sure he had no other wounds that needed care, but the rest of his body had only superficial cuts and bruises. Whatever had happened to him, the cause of this deep sleep was the wound in his chest.

And it looked even less deep than it had before. Kyne glanced up at the torch, but it shone with the same amount of light as it had when she hung it on the wall. And if it wasn't the light, that meant this unnamed boy was healing at an alarming rate, which was impossible...unless he wasn't what he seemed.

She stared down at his half-familiar face. His name hovered on the tip of her tongue, but she could not force it to the forefront of her mind. She would have to wait, perhaps until dawn, and see if sunlight named him.

If he woke up, she could attempt to get some answers, but she had a feeling he would be unconscious for quite some time. Until then, though, she could try to determine what had happened, contact Cynara, and wait.

Chapter 6

"Has there been any change?"

For the first time since he had arrived in Espen's house, the vampire thought she looked a bit tired. It wasn't anything in her voice or her manner; she exuded warmth and comfort just as much as before, but something had changed in the back of her gaze.

"He's still..." Asleep? Unconscious? He truly did not know. "He hasn't moved."

Indeed, Alban lay as if dead, save for the fact that the vampire's tenuous link to his twin had not been severed.

Espen placed one dark hand on his shoulder. "Come and get me as soon as he wakes up. Do you need anything?"

The vampire shook his head. "I'm fine."

Espen's silence reminded him of the way Skade had looked at him. He hesitated, wanting to ask, but not able to bear the thought of knowing she was dead. "Is..." He took a deep breath. "Is Skade..."

"She's alive, but only just," Espen said softly. "She spent the rest of her strength to save Nicodemus, and I haven't been able to find him yet."

"You could ask Zaira," the vampire whispered, for the little girl had helped him rescue Alban, after all.

Espen frowned. "Yes. I could. But I'd rather not."

The vampire smiled. "She doesn't mind."

"I know. But I do."

He heard her sigh as he turned his gaze back to Alban's slack face. "Call me as soon as he wakes up, okay?"

"I will."

The question he did not dare ask hung in the air between them, as loud as a scream. *What if he didn't wake up?* Terrin's spell had entwined his mind in many barbed layers. What if, by freeing Alban, the vampire had damaged his mind?

What if he never woke up? That specter haunted him even in sleep, and followed him down into dreams too deep for the horrors of his past to venture.

Chapter 7

It had taken Teluride a month to sit up without help, and another month to recover the use of his legs long enough to attempt to stand. The seizures had not returned since the last of Terrin's drugs were purged from his system, but the effects remained.

Every small step, every small achievement left him weak, but he knew he had to try if he wanted to think about the future.

At the moment, the future was a murky darkness in his mind, because he knew he was not strong enough to rule his inherited kingdom.

A King had to be able to tie his own shoes, after all.

He'd heard the commotion earlier, and Zaira had been kind enough to inform him of Espen's new guests. That Skade counted among the wounded tore at his heart.

Teluride had no great loyalty for the Queen of Iomar, but she *had* saved his life. And the world did not need to lose another Queen.

Dawn broke across the forest, and Teluride watched the sun rise, reluctant to crawl into bed. After lying in bed for so long, helpless to the whims of Terrin's drugs, he did not want to return to his bed unless he absolutely had to sleep.

He supposed it was a sign of his continued recovery that he was able to feel a bit bored.

The door opened behind him. Without looking, Teluride knew Zaira slipped through the crack; the heavy door had not opened wide enough to admit anyone else. She had taken to spending some time each day with him, but Teluride had never quite gotten up enough courage to ask her if she came at Espen's request or for some reason of her own.

"My father is dead," Zaira said softly.

Teluride turned, holding onto the windowsill for support. "You know this for certain?"

Zaira nodded. "I saw it happen."

Even though she had told him what her father had done to her, Teluride thought he saw the tracks of tears on her cheeks. "Have you told Espen?" He did not mention her tears.

"No." Zaira sighed and rubbed her bare arms. "She's busy with the others. I didn't want to bother her."

"I don't think you would be a bother," Teluride remarked. "Is...are they all still alive?"

Zaira nodded. "For now."

"And Nicodemus?" Gathering all his news secondhand had made Teluride learn which questions to ask and which to avoid. He felt a bit guilty using Zaira's talent like this, but she had assured him on more than one occasion that she didn't mind.

But just in case, he didn't tell Espen what he knew.

"I don't know," the little girl said. "I haven't Dreamed of him at all."

"Is he still a...a ghost?" He had almost said 'still alive'.

"He was. But I don't know where he is now." She sighed. "Espen said she tried to find him, but I don't think she tried too hard. And Nicodemus himself said he might not remember anything if he went into the mirror again."

Teluride could sympathize. Just remembering names and events took most of his strength on the bad days. He tried not to think about what would happen on bad days in the future, if things worked out the way they should.

"Thank you for telling me," he said.

Zaira smiled. "I don't want you to feel alone, Teluride. I know how you feel."

Teluride realized she *did* know how he felt. She had been locked in a tower for six years, after all. His own ordeal was nothing compared to hers.

"I still haven't asked you if I will regain my memory," he whispered. His memories contained only what he had been told, nothing more.

"Do you wish to ask me?" Zaira asked. "I can't answer you until you ask, you know."

Teluride swallowed hard. "I know. But there are more important things to ask, if I had only one chance to ask you a question."

"What would you ask if you only had one chance?" Zaira asked.

"Will we win?" Teluride asked after a moment of thought.

Zaira opened her mouth to answer him, then turned and ran from the room.

Teluride watched her go, both wary and puzzled by her behavior. In the end, he found he did not have enough strength to follow her, so he sank down on his bed and waited for enlightenment.

Chapter 8

At dawn, he still slept so deeply that his chest hardly rose and fell with each breath. At dusk, after Kyne spent the afternoon washing the blood from his body and finding him some clothing to wear, he stirred for the first time, but did not awaken.

All through the second night she watched him struggle with imaginary demons, torn by some unimaginable torment as he thrashed on the little bed. By noon on the second day, the wound in his chest was a dimple of pink flesh, nothing more. If Kyne had been asked, she would have had to say it looked to be years old, instead of days old.

Which was impossible, because no one could heal so quickly.

Four more days passed with no change, other than the continued healing of his wounds. Kyne debated whether to move him, but erred on the side of caution and left him on the cot. Although she itched to get back on the road, she knew she needed more information before she would be able to find Skade and the others. And right now, she had nothing to go on.

On the sixth morning, he opened his eyes. They were bloodshot and dazed, but Kyne thought she saw a hint of awareness amid the pain. She waited for him to speak, but he just stared.

"You've been asleep for many days," she finally said. "I found you here six days ago."

He licked cracked lips and opened his mouth. "My Queen?"

As soon as he spoke, Kyne knew why he had seemed so familiar. She had seen him before, after all, in Leysan, but not alive. No, not alive. A ghost. *Skade's* ghost.

"I was rather hoping you would tell me that," Kyne said. "Do you remember what happened?"

He erupted from the bed, one hand closed around her wrist before she could even consider reaching for her sword. His muscles shook with the effort of rising, but he did not fall.

"He...I have to warn them!" His eyes rolled up into the back of his head. "I..." He choked on the rest of the sentence and fell back. His grip relaxed, his fingers slipped away from Kyne's arm.

Kyne waited to see if he would awaken, but his eyes remained closed, his breathing ragged, as if something worse than the wound that had so quickly vanished from his chest sapped both strength and will.

What had Skade called him? "Mirror?"

His breath hitched. "I know my name now."

"What is it?" Kyne kept her voice soft.

"N...Nicodemus." He licked his lips again. A trickle of bright blood spilled out of the side of his mouth, and Kyne wondered if he'd bitten his tongue.

She wiped the blood away. "Well, then, Nicodemus. Do you remember me?"

One side of his mouth twitched, as if he struggled not to smile. "How could I forget? You were with...Alban and the vampire. Here."

"Yes."

"I remember you."

"Do you know what happened?" She hated to press him, but she had to find out. For both her Queen and her own curiosity, if truth be told. She did not want to find out she'd made a mistake leaving Alban with Skade, after all.

But instead of answering her, he opened his eyes and tried to rise again. Kyne pushed him back down.

"Do you have a horse?" His voice cracked. "I must..."

"You must rest, or you *will* die," Kyne said firmly. "I'm not sure how you managed to heal from that wound so quickly, but you're in no shape to travel."

Nicodemus stared at her. "You don't understand. I have to warn them."

"Warn who?" Kyne did not pull away when he grabbed her arm again, but this time, as she watched his eyes roll back in his head, she realized he was not merely exhausted. Something, some wound she had overlooked, or something worse, sapped his strength and left him weak in its grasp. But what had happened to him?

This time, he spoke through clenched teeth and his grip on her arm did not lessen. "If I say Terrin's spell, do you know what I'm talking about?"

"No," Kyne said. "I know he had a spell over Alban, but..."

"Ten years ago, Terrin loosed a spell over Cruinne," Nicodemus whispered, then grimaced. "No, it wasn't just Terrin. I helped him. And so did Skade's son, Michael. And Cathan..." He whimpered. "I have to warn them..."

"Tell me about the spell," Kyne urged, figuring he would get to the point eventually.

He took a deep breath and choked a little, but managed to continue. "The spell was more like a magical virus. It...thrived on power. Any use of power would make it more deadly. Skade and Espen managed to quarantine those we infected, but Terrin escaped."

"You didn't," Kyne said. That explained why he had been Skade's prisoner, but not why he was now alive.

"No. But Skade saved my life. Terrin infected me soon after we were caught."

Kyne wanted to snatch her arm away from his grasp, but she hesitated. Surely, if the spell--or whatever it was--was highly contagious, more people would have been infected. And there would have been no way for the mainland not to catch wind of what had happened.

"You can't catch it unless the spell is spoken and there are...certain ingredients that must come in contact with your blood," Nicodemus whispered. "But..."

Through fits and starts, he managed to tell her what had happened to Skade and the others. Kyne felt ill just thinking about Alban in his father's hands again. But even if she *had* taken him to Severin, would Cynara's protections have kept Terrin out? Or would he have found a way to take his son despite them?

"You're certain Skade was infected?" That explained why everyone in Iomar claimed their Queen was not missing. Kyne wondered if they even knew.

"Yes." Nicodemus closed his eyes. It was more than obvious that the telling had exhausted what reserves of strength he had left. If she had not seen the wound in his chest healing before her eyes, Kyne would have doubted he would live through the night.

"And what is it you have to warn her about?" Kyne asked. "Is Terrin planning to attack Skade?"

"Skade is safe in Espen's house," Nicodemus whispered. "But...but Cathan is wearing my face. I have to warn..."

At least he didn't try to rise this time, Kyne thought. Aloud, she asked, "Who is Cathan?"

"He is a shifter," Nicodemus whispered. "The rarest of talents, even rarer than a Dreamer. He can assume the identity of anyone, and he is wearing my face."

"He's planning to find Espen's house and attack Skade there?"

"He's planning to get inside Espen's wards and open the way for Terrin to attack," Nicodemus whispered. "Now, do you see why I must warn them?" But there was no heat in his words this time. And his face had paled even further, save for the smudged shadows beneath his eyes. Even his eyelids looked bruised.

"This Espen..." Kyne began.

"She's a Healer," Nicodemus whispered.

"Do you know where she lives?" Kyne had heard of the vast network of Healers, of course, but she had never met one.

Nicodemus' lips twitched again. "A piece of me...of my spirit...is trapped in a crystal Cathan carries with him. I will be able to track him."

"But you won't be able to get to Espen's house before he does," Kyne said, not liking this plan.

"I have no strength to form a portal," Nicodemus whispered. Tears tracked down both sides of his face, as if he knew full well that their only hope had close to no chance of success.

"If you had the strength, where would you go?" Kyne asked.

Nicodemus opened his eyes. "Ask me where Espen lives," he whispered.

"Where does Espen live?" Kyne was more than happy to oblige, but she hadn't realized he was a Dreamer.

"Her cottage lies in the forest outside Aberdus," Nicodemus whispered. More tears trickled down his cheeks. "Ask me...no." He opened his eyes and managed a small smile. "There are some things I'd rather not know."

Like if his Queen would live, Kyne thought, *or if he would succeed in warning them before Cathan struck.* She didn't really blame him for not wanting to know, but she thought that even if he Dreamed he would fail, he would try anyway, just to make the effort to prove himself wrong.

"I will come with you," she said.

Nicodemus nodded. "I'd hoped you would."

She could do no less, in truth. It was quite obvious that she had erred in leaving Alban and the vampire in Iomar, and if she could rectify her mistake by saving their lives, she would.

"I have a horse, but I doubt you can ride," she said. "I could make a litter, and pull you behind..."

Nicodemus' eyes glinted. "I will ride."

"If you kill yourself before we arrive, you'll be in no position to help your Queen," Kyne said gently.

"I know." Even though his voice was thick with resignation, he managed to smile at her again. "I don't want to die again, Kyne. I want you to know that. I don't want to die again, but I will if I have to." He said this last part with such feeling that Kyne half-expected him to rise from his bed and walk out of the room.

Which was ridiculous, because even though the wound in his chest had healed, Terrin's spell still sapped his strength. "I know."

In truth, that was the only thing she could say and not feel pretentious.

Two hours later, with Nicodemus on a sturdy litter dragged behind her horse, they were on their way.

And, although she realized it would be a miracle if they got to Espen's house before Cathan, she could only hope that they would not be too late.

Chapter 9

Breathing hard, Zaira ducked down behind a bush in the garden and tried to forget what she has seen. *Teluride's face, bloody and pale, his eyes staring sightlessly into oblivion. Beside him, Alban, burned almost beyond recognition. And curled up next to Alban, Zaira herself, pale hair red with blood...and dead.*

This was not the first time she'd Dreamed of her own death, nor would it be the last. But this Dream was different. This Dream held no solution, just a promise of the future, as if nothing she would do mattered.

She had to find out how to prevent what she had seen. She *had* to. She had grown rather fond of Teluride since he came to convalesce in Espen's cottage, and she didn't want him to die. She didn't want Alban to die, either. In fact, she would prefer this whole horror to be over and done with so she could Dream of a future with much less chaos.

To prevent what she had seen, she would have to get someone to ask her a very specific question. Her first inclination was to ask the vampire, but she really didn't want to bother him. He had a lot on his mind with Alban, after all. And he hadn't been in her Dream.

Of course, that could mean he was already dead in her Dream, but she doubted that. She had a feeling that the vampire would be very difficult for Terrin to kill.

She had no second inclination. She didn't want to ask Teluride, because he would demand to know why she'd run from the answer to his question. Espen would refuse to ask it, and both Alban and Skade were unconscious.

That left Skade's son, Michael, or Enapay. Zaira thought Enapay might ask her the question, but she wasn't sure she could get to the little girl without Michael's knowledge.

And that narrowed it down to Michael. Zaira slipped back into the house and padded down the hall to the room Espen had given Skade's son. She found him asleep, curled up in his blankets like a much younger boy, his brow furrowed and his breathing labored.

"Michael?" When she touched his shoulder, he jerked awake and stared at her through sleep-blurred eyes.

He coughed. "Zaira?"

"I need you to ask me a question, Michael." She tried to keep the impatience out of her voice.

He blinked at her, then slowly sat up, rubbing his arm. "A question?"

"Teluride asked me a question, but what I saw *cannot* happen," Zaira said. "I don't want anyone else to die."

Michael's eyes cleared. "That's right. You're a prophet."

"Terrin called me his Dreamer," Zaira said. "And I need you to ask me a question."

Michael hesitated. "What question?"

"How can I stop what I saw?" Zaira asked. Not for the first time, she wished she could ask herself questions and have the answers appear in her mind. That luxury would make things so much easier.

"How can you stop what you saw?" Michael repeated.

Nothing happened. Zaira blinked. She had never *not* gotten an answer to a question.

"Ask me again," she commanded.

"How can you stop what you saw?" Michael asked.

Zaira's eyes filled with tears. She would have rushed out of Michael's room to hide in the garden again, but Michael gently took her arm and knelt in front of her.

"What did you see?"

Zaira hiccoughed a sob. "It doesn't matter. I can't stop what I saw. If I could, I would have Dreamed a solution when you asked me."

"What did you see?" Michael wouldn't release her arm.

"Death," Zaira whispered.

Michael's grip tightened. "My mother?"

Of course he would think of his mother first, Zaira thought. "No. Alban. Teluride. And...and...me."

"Oh, I see." Michael sat back on his heels and released her. "Well, if you can't stop what you saw, can anyone else?"

Zaira stared at him. Why hadn't *she* thought to ask that question? "Yes!" She almost shouted the words. "Yes." Now she knew she had made the right decision to come to Michael.

"Good." Zaira was certain he meant his smile to be reassuring, but he didn't quite pull it off. "So who...who can stop what you saw?" The expression on his face told her that he had already guessed the answer to that question.

Zaira considered what little she knew about him. He had done a horrible thing to be exiled, yes, but he had also proven himself trustworthy in his new life. She didn't think he would refuse to help them.

"You can," she said, keeping her voice soft.

Michael reacted without even considering her words. "No way. I have responsibilities. I'm a..."

"You're a member of a Council that balances the mundane and the supernatural world," Zaira said. "I know."

Michael folded his arms in front of his chest. "What else do you *know* about me?" It was a question, and he realized it a second after he spoke. "Wait."

Zaira opened her mouth to tell him, saw the anguish in his gaze, and decided to take pity on him--this time. "I know you have to abide by certain rules to be a member of the Council," she whispered. "And one of those rules..."

Michael sighed. "Is to not refuse a plea for help. Yes, I know."

"Are things so different here?" Zaira asked. "Wouldn't you like to remove the threat of Terrin's spell and find the cure?" *Wouldn't you like your mother to live?*

Michael rubbed one hand across his face. "You don't understand. I...I was exiled." It was a weak argument, and they both knew it. "I have a family now. And I can't abandon my duties as a member of the Council."

"But you can contact them here, and tell them what's going on," Zaira said. "Surely they would understand."

The look in his eyes told her that they would understand for more than one reason, but he did not speak.

"If you don't help us, Teluride, Alban, and I will die."

"And if I help you no one will die?" Michael asked, his voice harsh. "I can't believe that."

"My Dreams change due to actions I did not foresee," Zaira said. "What happens now will begin the thread for the end of this, Michael. That much I *do* know."

Michael shook his head and turned away.

Zaira pressed on, unwilling to let him refuse. "If you agree to help, the future will be brighter. If you don't, I can see no way around our deaths."

"I don't want anyone to die," Michael said.

"I don't either." Zaira waited to see if he would add anything more, but he remained silent, his head bowed. "I'm sorry, Michael. If I could see it any other way..." She turned to go. Her Dreams had been quite plain as to what would happen if Michael refused to help. She had no other options left to stave off death.

His voice stopped her at the door. "Will my mother live, Zaira?"

For a moment, Zaira contemplated telling him that Skade would live if he agreed to help them, but she couldn't bring herself to be so cruel.

"Yes, she will." She glanced back at him as she spoke, and saw a knot of tension release from his shoulders.

"Good."

Mired in despair, Zaira turned to leave the room. Her hand was on the doorknob before Michael spoke again.

"I'll stay." His voice was so soft that she almost missed his words.

"What?" Hope made her voice crack.

Michael turned. "I'll stay. I'll help you finish this."

Zaira's eyes filled with tears. Too overcome with joy to speak, she sank to her knees and sobbed into Michael's chest when he knelt to cradle her in his arms.

"Thank you," she blubbered.

Michael's voice shook a little. "You're welcome."

Zaira heard him whisper, "I hope you're right," but he didn't phrase it as a question, so she could not reassure him.

Yet.

Chapter 10

Skade opened her eyes. For a moment, she had no inkling of where she lay or why she felt so weak, but memory would not allow her to wallow in ignorance for long.

Her first thought was for Nicodemus, her second for her son.

Once, she would have thought of Michael first, but ten years had changed her perspective of him. Ten years had changed everyone quite a bit.

Skade raised her hand, marveling that it still obeyed her command. She knew without a doubt that Espen had saved her life; by rights she should be dead.

Others had died after using half the amount of magic she had used, victims of Terrin's spell. Why, then, had she lived?

"I'm not sure," Espen said from her seat beside Skade's bed. "You should be dead."

Skade licked her lips. "I know." She did not mention that she hadn't spoken her question aloud; Espen would deny reading her mind, but the truth remained. "Michael?"

"He's here." Espen's voice was so neutral Skade could have used it as a level. "He's very worried about you."

Skade managed a smile, but it was short-lived. "*I'm* very worried about me."

"How do you feel?" Espen leaned forward and rested her elbows on her knees.

Skade considered her question very carefully. "Weak."

"That's to be expected," Espen said. "And if you have any outstanding spells that I haven't found and put in stasis, I suggest you release them now."

Skade struggled to think. Her first inclination was to release every active spell, but what about the Sleepers? If she released that spell, they would die.

"I've taken care of the Sleepers," Espen said. "Are there any others?"

"None that can't be shunted to someone else," Skade whispered. "Most are self-sustaining. They won't miss me."

"What about your kingdom?" Espen asked. "Do I need to contact anyone?"

"My maids know what to do," Skade said. "Use the mirror in my room. Someone will be there waiting for my contact."

"And what should I tell them?" Espen asked.

Skade closed her eyes. "Tell them I've been...detained and that I'll be home soon."

"And if you *won't* be home soon?"

Skade sighed. "I am not already dead." She tried to glare.

Espen laughed softly. "Now you're looking more like yourself. That's a relief."

Skade couldn't help but smile; laughter was a bit beyond her strength. "You haven't mentioned Nicodemus."

"That's because I don't know what happened to him," Espen said. "He didn't respond when I tried to contact him."

"He could have been in shock," Skade whispered.

"You put him in a mirror that housed an open portal," Espen said. "In truth, he could be anywhere."

Skade had not thought of that. In the heat of the moment, she had used the only available mirror. And Nicodemus would have to suffer the consequences.

"Can you look for him when you have a moment?" she asked. "He *did* save my life, for what that's worth."

"I'll look for him right after I contact your...maids," Espen said. "Do you need anything at the moment?"

"I'm fine," Skade whispered, and closed her eyes. "But I do want to see my son."

"I'll send him in."

Skade nodded, but didn't open her eyes. Although her body was weak, her mind raced through various possibilities, trying to pinpoint where Nicodemus might be. What to do next. How to stop Terrin this time, before he infected the entire world and left himself ruler over a graveyard.

And how to survive this. That was the most important thought of all, really, but Skade couldn't believe that Terrin's spell would kill her. She couldn't die. Not now, not after discovering Michael's innocence. Not after thwarting Terrin this far.

Sleep dragged her down into darkness. She did not fight its strength.

Chapter 11

In the end, it was easier than Cathan thought to slip inside Espen's wards. All he had to do was find her cottage--a simple task, really--then bide his time and wait.

He had stolen a cloak from Leysan, and it hid his identity as he slipped between the trees that surrounded Espen's home. He had taken pains not to meet anyone on his way, even though the pain of his wounds and gnawing hunger did force him to venture close to outlying farms once or twice. He supposed stale bread would sustain him until he could rest in Espen's care, provided she didn't see through his ruse immediately.

But no one had seen through his shiftings before. Why should they now? He had copied Nicodemus' body exactly, from the paleness of his skin to his scars.

He would have to stay away from Michael's brat, of course. Even though she hadn't had much interaction with Nicodemus, she might see through his seeming. And he didn't want his careful plan to be destroyed by a six-year-old child.

His strength gave out at the edge of Espen's wards. He collapsed against a tree and waited, certain the witch would feel his pain and find him.

After a little while, the pain grew too much to bear, and he slipped away into darkness, confident that his seeming would not shift, even now. He had been Michael on more than one occasion, after all, and he had not slipped then. Now, even wounded, his subconscious realized this form had to endure if he would see Terrin triumph.

Chapter 12

Restless, Zaira slipped out into the garden again, more to avoid everyone else than for solace. Even with Michael's agreement to stay, she still didn't feel reassured that her Dream would not come true.

Sometimes...most times...she wished she were just a normal little girl instead of a Dreamer.

She was out in the garden for fifteen minutes before she saw the crumpled form at the edge of the forest. For a moment, she thought that it was a trick of Terrin's, but the figure lay still enough to be dead.

If she had been more cautious, she would have run back into the house and told Espen what she saw, but she did not want to disturb the witch's work on Skade. She had told Michael his mother would not die, but she did not know how she would live.

Keeping close to the trees that dotted the garden, Zaira slowly approached the shrouded form. When it didn't move, she grew less cautious. By the time she reached the edge of the garden, she didn't bother to hide behind the trees.

The figure never moved. When Zaira grew close enough to pull back its hood, she hesitated, all her old fears returning with a vengeance.

If this were a trap, she had already sprung it. And she could not leave a wounded person lying in the forest, even for five minutes.

She touched the sodden cloak and pulled away the hood. When she saw who lay beneath it, she forgot all her fears and misgivings; forgot everything but the impossibility of who lay bloody and unconscious, on Espen's doorstep.

Zaira dropped to her knees. "Nicodemus?"

Behind her, she heard Espen's familiar footsteps. Zaira glanced over her shoulder. "It's Nicodemus!"

Espen nodded. "I see that. And I doubt I have to warn you not to step outside the garden again." The Healer knelt beside Nicodemus. Her hands immediately began to glow, but after a moment, she frowned.

"What's wrong? Is he dead?" Zaira's voice dropped. Skade would be crushed if Nicodemus had returned from the dead only to die alone.

"No. He's alive, but very weak. But I thought..." Espen shook her head. "Perhaps I missed something from the other side of the mirror. I thought he had been stabbed."

"Maybe Terrin missed," Zaira suggested.

Espen's frown deepened, but she did not remove her hands from Nicodemus' body. "Perhaps."

But she didn't ask Zaira, so she would not know for certain.

Five minutes after she appeared in the garden, Espen gathered Nicodemus up into her arms. She left his cloak behind. And from seeing the blood on his clothes, Zaira didn't blame her.

Espen vanished into an empty room with Nicodemus, leaving Zaira to her own designs. After finding Nicodemus back from the dead, Zaira didn't want to go back to her room, so she stayed in the kitchen, staring out at the garden until the sun set and put the entire forest in shadow.

Chapter 13

Two days after they left Leysan, Kyne abandoned the litter. Even traveling on the road, it was slow going, and the amount of time she spent trying to force her horse to bear an unsteady weight only added to time they did not truly have.

So she hoisted Nicodemus up on the horse in front of her, and because he weighed so little, her horse did not mind the added burden.

"I have to warn them..."

Their goal was a litany, murmured over and over under his breath until he did not have breath to repeat it. And Terrin's spell left him so weak he could hardly hold up his head at times.

To get to Aberdus, they had to travel perilously close to Glinyeu. And knowing what she knew about Eabon and his loyalties, she should have known to be on guard.

They had stopped for the night off the side of the road, and Nicodemus thrashed in the throes of dreams as Kyne kept watch. But constant vigilance takes its toll, and she had only closed her eyes for a moment when the point of a sword pricked her throat.

Nicodemus did not awaken when two silent men lifted him up, and Kyne had no choice but to submit to them if she wanted to win him back. She could have fought them, yes, but both men and their mounts looked fresh, and Kyne had been on the road for too many days.

"We meant no trespass," she said. "We're on our way to Aberdus. I wanted to take my friend to a Healer there."

One of the men nodded, as if he did not fault her judgment. "We've been instructed to take all travelers to see our King," he said. "I'm sorry, my lady, but at least you'll sleep dry for a night. And the castle isn't much further down the road."

Whatever reason Eabon gave for wanting to see every traveler on the road had to have something to do with Terrin. And if Terrin had fled Leysan, where else could he have gone?

They did not bind her hands, and they did not search her for weapons or make her give up her sword. By the time they reached the castle, Kyne saw why: a veritable crowd of people sat or stood in the castle hall, guarded by dour-faced men who no doubt longed for their own beds. Evidently, the roads surrounding Glinyeu were populous indeed.

Peasants sat beside lords and ladies, all of whom looked extremely put out at this outrage. With a growing sense of unease, Kyne sat beside Nicodemus and listened to the flow of conversations around her. Some of the travelers had been held here for *days*.

"Kyne." Nicodemus spoke without opening his eyes.

"I'm right here," Kyne whispered. "We're in Glinyeu. Do you know what's going on?"

Nicodemus' breath hissed from between clenched teeth. The closest travelers glanced their way, and seeing how ill Nicodemus looked, moved away.

Kyne preferred to be left alone. "Tell me what you see, Nicodemus. Why is Eabon taking people from the roads?"

Nicodemus opened his eyes. For the first time since he awoke, fear pushed past the pain of Terrin's spell. "You have to flee."

"I'm not going anywhere without you," Kyne said.

"You have to go." Nicodemus clutched her arm. "Eabon is dead." His voice rose on the last word, and a couple of people glanced at them curiously.

"Then who is giving the orders?" Kyne asked, but she already suspected the answer.

"Terrin. He intends...he wants to flush Skade and Espen out of hiding. He wants his sons back." Nicodemus shuddered. "And he has a secret weapon."

"His spell." Kyne stared at the people around her and wondered if anyone suspected they were about to die. "He's going to unleash his spell on all of these people?"

"Those with power will die," Nicodemus whispered. "The weaker ones will die first; probably the first time they use their talents. Terrin will drink the power of their passing to become stronger."

"That's barbarous," Kyne whispered, appalled.

"I think..." Nicodemus stared at a distant set of doors and shook his head. "I think he's forgotten his original goal. I think now he will stop at nothing to see Skade dead--and Alban and Alexander helpless slaves."

"But Skade's already infected," Kyne whispered. "All he has to do is bide his time."

"Terrin's patience has run out," Nicodemus said. "And he plans to act soon. If you don't flee, you'll die just like everyone else."

"What will happen to you?" Kyne asked. It was true that she'd be able to slip out unnoticed easier if she were alone, but she hadn't brought Nicodemus out of Leysan to leave him alone with Terrin.

Nicodemus shuddered again. "I...I think I..."

The particulars of Terrin's spell rose up in her mind. "Wait, Nicodemus. You told me the use of magic made the spell work faster."

"Yes." His voice was very faint.

"The use of any talent?"

He closed his eyes. "Yes."

"Damn it! Why didn't you..." Kyne bit off what would be her seventh question and scowled. "You should have told me. Reminded me. I thought you were getting better." It was difficult not asking questions that would force him to Dream.

"I'm sorry." His limp fingers twitched, but he couldn't summon up enough strength to move them.

"No, I'm the one who should be sorry," Kyne said. "And I'm still not leaving you here."

"You have to."

"No, I don't." Kyne coaxed him into a sitting position and slung one of his arms around her shoulder. "We're leaving together." She wished she could warn the others, but what good would it do? Short of murdering Terrin now... She let Nicodemus slide down to the floor and lowered herself beside him.

"You've thought of something?" At least *he* could ask questions without repercussions.

"I have. I know that you know what I am for my sister."

"Yes." Was his voice growing a bit stronger, or was that just wishful thinking?

She would give her life to see Terrin gone, after all. He threatened the whole of Cruinne, and she wanted the peace her sister craved.

"I'm going to put you on my horse," Kyne said. "You're going to ride to Aberdus and warn Espen." Her tone brooked no room for arguments.

Nicodemus opened his eyes. "What are you going to do?"

Kyne doubted she could surprise him, but she doubted he had Dreamed of this. "I'm going to end this," she said. "End this or die trying."

Nicodemus shook his head. "No. Not yet. You'll fail."

"You know this for a fact," Kyne snapped, not liking his declaration.

"Yes, I do. You'll fail. You can't kill him yet."

"It would make it so much easier if I could," Kyne said. "What about everyone else here? I don't want to walk away and leave them to die, Nicodemus."

The question was purely rhetorical, and she didn't realize she'd asked it until Nicodemus' eyes rolled back into his head again. He collapsed, gasping, and a trickle of blood ran from both his mouth and his nose.

This time, he didn't respond. His eyes remained closed; his breathing so faint that Kyne had to bend over him to make sure he still lived.

If he died, it would be her fault, after all. She could have chosen her words with more care.

"Nicodemus..."

"Nicodemus?" A new voice intruded on her guilt, and she cursed herself again for her inattention. "Surely not."

Kyne knew who would stand above her even before she raised her head. "Your spell is killing him, Terrin. What is the antidote?"

"Wouldn't you like to know?" Terrin smirked. He beckoned to two of the guards. "Bring them both. And make sure to strip the girl of her weapons.

She'll have plenty of them." He strode back into the shadows before Kyne could deliver a parting shot.

This time, the guards--and there were more than two now--stripped her of her weapons, save a hidden dagger, and left them in a pile on the floor. This time, they lifted Nicodemus with a bit more care, but bound her hands and pushed her along with him.

The guards took them to a smaller room and lay Nicodemus against one wall. Kyne sat beside him, feeling horribly out of place. She had not pledged to protect him, no, but even then, she *had* pledged to get him to Aberdus. And she had failed.

Fifteen minutes after the guards left them, Terrin appeared, looking none the worse for wear. He ignored Kyne and dragged Nicodemus to the other side of the room. When repeated shaking did not awaken him, he turned to Kyne with fire in his eyes.

"What did you do to him?"

"I asked him a question," Kyne said. "Inadvertently, after I realized what my questions were doing to him."

Terrin frowned. "Even so, he shouldn't be so deeply unconscious. It only took Zaira two weeks to recover from my spell. How long has he been like this? I thought he was dead."

Kyne didn't know how much to tell Terrin without betraying Nicodemus' plan. "I don't know. My sister sent me to try to discern what had happened in Leysan, and I found him there. He's been in and out of consciousness ever since." Perhaps if she played dumb, he would believe her.

Terrin's lip curled. "What did he tell you?"

Kyne shrugged. "Not much. Something about Skade...and I gathered there was some sort of explosion. I didn't even recognize him until he spoke to me. I've never seen him alive."

"That's right. You went back to report to your sister, didn't you?" Terrin smiled. "Did you tell her what my son did while he had you trapped?"

Kyne felt a surge of anger that had nothing to do with her present situation. She'd purposely blocked most of those memories from her mind, and had even gone so far as to refuse to tell Cynara what had happened. In truth, what had happened was between her and Alban alone, and he didn't even remember what he had done.

Evidently, Terrin did. Or was he fishing for information? Had his control over Alban been so complete?

"And what is it that you think he did?" Kyne asked. "I remember every second that I was under his control, Terrin. And even *you* cannot force a good person to become like you."

"My son is more like me than he thinks." Terrin dismissed Alban's moral standing with a shrug. "Nicodemus, open your eyes."

Nicodemus remained mute; dead to the world, even though Kyne hated to use that analogy. And then, seconds after Terrin's order, he shuddered and gasped in a breath. His eyes fluttered open; he saw Terrin's face and froze.

"So nice of you to join us, Nicodemus." Terrin crouched down in front of his prisoner, turning his back to Kyne.

She tensed. With only a dagger left, she would have only one chance to strike. And even then, her odds of escaping from the castle were next to nil. Unless Nicodemus had enough strength to form a portal, which she doubted, they would have to get past all the guards *and* find her horse, which would leave very little time for the possibility of a mistake.

Nicodemus licked his lips. "Where is my Queen?"

"I would hope that she is dead by now," Terrin replied. "But no doubt she's managed to live. Your Queen has been curiously difficult to kill."

"I think...she...will live," Nicodemus whispered. He coughed and a trickle of blood spilled out over his lips.

"I think you're wrong," Terrin said. "Where is she now?"

Nicodemus moaned, but did not slip into unconsciousness at the question. "You already know. In Espen's cottage. Safe."

"And my sons? Are both my sons there as well?"

"Yes."

Kyne supposed that since these questions merely reiterated what Terrin already knew, they would not hurt Nicodemus as badly. But she had no doubt that Terrin would continue the questioning until Nicodemus lost consciousness--or died.

"I'll...wait to ask you the most pertinent questions," Terrin said. "I *do* want you to live, after all. But there is one I must ask: Zaira recovered from my spell. Will you?"

Nicodemus did not respond for a long time. At first, Kyne thought he was unconscious again, but he opened his eyes when Terrin reached out to shake him awake.

"Yes." His voice was almost too low for Kyne to hear. "Yes, I will recover."

"Good." Terrin stood. "It's a shame, you know, that you gave your loyalty to Skade. We could have worked together."

"I'm sorry I ever trusted you," Nicodemus whispered.

Terrin kicked him. Nicodemus gasped and tried to roll away, but the wall blocked any defensive movement.

Kyne struggled to her knees as Terrin kicked him again. "Terrin! He may survive your spell, but he won't survive if you kick him to death."

Terrin scowled and glared at her. "Mind your own business, meddler," he spat. "I'd kill you now, but I've yet to recover from Skade's spells. I need more power."

"You won't have enough power to break through Espen's wards, even if you kill everyone in Glinyeu," Nicodemus whispered.

Terrin smiled down at him. "I don't have to," he said. "I only need enough power to reactivate the spell I placed on Alban. He will do the work for me."

"Hasn't he suffered enough?" Kyne spat.

"No, he hasn't," Terrin said. "He is mine. They both are mine to do with what I will."

"You can't own someone else like that," Nicodemus whispered.

"Ah, but there you're wrong," Terrin said. "Skade owns *you*, after all, or she did while she held you in the mirror. How will she react to see you alive again, Nicodemus? Will she imprison you?"

Kyne couldn't fault his logic, for it was perfectly true. Skade *had* owned Nicodemus while he was her prisoner in the mirror. He'd had no free will, at least not that Kyne had seen.

Nicodemus was silent, mulling this over.

"She brainwashed you," Terrin said. "She stole your memories and your will, and forced you to become her servant."

"Yes, you're right," Nicodemus whispered.

"Don't listen to him, Nicodemus," Kyne said, anger riding her words. "He's trying to confuse you. He's trying to make you doubt your intentions."

"I'm telling him the truth, and even *you* cannot fault my words," Terrin said. "Skade raped his mind."

"But my Queen..." Wounded as he was, Kyne had no difficulty believing Nicodemus would succumb to Terrin's point of view eventually. And if Terrin managed to turn Nicodemus against Skade, Kyne did not know what the Iomarian Queen would do. She had spared Nicodemus' life once. Would she do so again?

"Nicodemus." Kyne kept her voice firm. "Don't listen to him."

"Perhaps I should take you to a more comfortable room," Terrin suggested, ignoring her. "You could rest in comfort if you agreed to at least consider my proposal."

"Your proposal?" Nicodemus asked.

"I've lost Zaira," Terrin said, and Kyne wondered if she should remind Nicodemus where Terrin had kept Zaira for six years. "I am in need of a prophet's aid. You helped me before...why don't you forget your Queen and help me again?"

"No," Nicodemus whispered. "I can't abandon my Queen."

"She isn't your Queen," Terrin said, anger finally showing in his voice. "She abandoned you in Leysan."

"She..." Kyne opened her mouth to shout him down, but Nicodemus was not so far gone as to tell Terrin everything. "She thought I was dead."

"As did I," Terrin said. "And now that you are not, please consider my request." Before Nicodemus could deny him again, he turned on his heel and stalked from the room.

Kyne half-expected a parting shot before he left, but he did not distinguish her with even a glare.

The door slammed shut; the lock engaged. And they were left alone, no closer to their goal.

Chapter 14

After Zaira left, Espen had come with the news that Skade had awakened. Michael felt more anxiety than joy at the news, especially after Espen informed him that Skade had asked to see him.

He wanted to feel excited, happy, even, but he could not shake the low-grade dread that seemed to have taken up residence in his soul. But if she had asked for him, he could not deny her, so he left his room for the first time since he entered it, checked in on Enapay, who was still asleep, and walked the short distance to where his mother lay.

She looked so fragile under the shelter of one of Espen's colorful quilts, but even the bright colors brought no roses to her pale cheeks. Michael sat in the chair beside her bed and waited, content to just see her without the specter of his exile hanging over every word in their future conversation.

Zaira *had* said she would live, but what if Zaira was wrong? Michael knew from long experience that prophets were not infallible. In fact, he had long believed that Nicodemus himself hadn't seen--or had chosen to ignore--the warning signs of Terrin's madness in his Dreams. They had been so stupid; drunk on the power of youth, and it had destroyed each of them.

It was so quiet in Skade's room. Michael passed the time just listening to his mother's every breath, tensing for that moment where she would no longer breathe. He closed his eyes and lost himself in worry of what would happen next. He had yet to contact the Council and tell them where he was, and no doubt Lucas was frantic with worry by now. But contacting the Council paled in comparison to waiting for his mother to die.

"I'm not dead yet," Skade whispered.

Michael opened his eyes. For a moment, he could not bring himself to speak. He stared into her familiar gaze and tried to fight back the tears that threatened to consume him. "I'm glad of that," he said, hardly able to speak past the lump in his throat.

"How is your daughter?" Skade asked.

"She's asleep." Michael was almost happy she did not venture into uncharted territory right away. "I think she'll be fine."

"And her mother?"

"I love her mother very much," Michael said. Which was the truth.

"Does she love you?" Skade smiled when he hesitated. "You don't have to tell me, Michael. I saw from the picture in Enapay's room. Where did you meet her?"

Michael cleared his throat. "She...she rescued me from Hell." That sentence neatly summed up twenty years of torment, but the truth of the story came nowhere near a simple declaration. "A lot has happened to me in twenty-eight years, mother."

Skade nodded. "I imagine so." Her fingers twitched on top of the quilt, and Michael slowly took her hand, marveling at the coolness of her touch. Skade's grip tightened. "You're staying here with us? To see this through?"

"I promised Zaira I would stay," Michael said. "So, I will. And since Sarah's in England, I guess Enapay will stay here as well." He didn't care for that part of the plan. Enapay should be somewhere safe, not with him in the midst of battle.

"I would like to see my granddaughter again." Skade's eyes glittered in the dim light of the only lamp in the room. "Will you bring her to me when she wakes up?"

"Of course," Michael promised. He could not deny her, not now.

"And then...Michael, I want you to promise me you'll send her away." Skade used Michael's grip as leverage to pull herself up. "Promise me. Whatever will happen, this is no place for a child."

"I will." Even though he hated to leave her out of his sight, he knew his mother was right. He could not take Enapay everywhere. And if he died, then at least Sarah would have something to remember him by.

The thought must have shone on his face, for Skade squeezed his hand again. "You won't die."

"You don't know that," Michael said. "You're no prophet."

"You're right, but when you were born, I asked a prophet about you," Skade said. "And he said...he said you would live a long and interesting life."

"Depending on whom you ask, I've lived long enough for two..."

Skade twisted her hand out of his grasp and touched his arm. "Michael, you *don't* want to make me mad. Not now."

It was a bald reminder of his status here, and Michael had to push away bitter resentment before he could speak clearly. "Then should I call you 'My Queen' like Nicodemus did?"

As soon as he mentioned Nicodemus' name, he realized he should have kept his mouth shut. Skade squeezed her eyes shut, as if Terrin's spell had taken a bit more strength than she could afford to lose. The anger deserted him as quickly as it had come. He sank down on his knees and buried his head in the folds of Espen's quilt.

"I'm sorry." He wanted to say so much; to beg for her forgiveness, but even now, years of lies--Cathan's lies--still ruled his emotions. "I'm so sorry. I failed you."

Movement must have cost her dearly, but Skade managed to sit up and wrap her arms around his shoulders. "Hush. I think we're both at fault, Michael." She stroked his hair, but he hardly felt her touch.

"I should have..." They both spoke at once. Michael tensed, then raised his head to stare at his mother. "I should have trusted you," he whispered.

"And I should have paid more attention to my only son," Skade said. "We were *both* at fault."

"You shouldn't be sitting up," Michael said in alarm. "You should rest. I should have let you rest."

"Michael." This time, she put one finger over his mouth to stop the flow of words. "I feel as fine as I am able. I'm not going to die just yet. Please, believe me."

She sounded stronger, somehow. Michael did not understand it, but his memories were riddled with the sick and the dying; and those who had perished when Terrin lost control and Michael's paltry healing powers were exhausted.

"At least lie down," he begged, and she acquiesced gracefully, sinking down into the support of pillows that he propped up around her. "And allow me to apologize for losing my temper."

Skade smiled. "I think you were provoked, and if I must accept your apology, I insist you accept mine."

"As you wish," Michael said, seeing no way to convince her she wasn't at fault. "Should I leave you to rest? Or would you like to...talk?"

"I'd like very much to talk to you, Michael," Skade whispered. "I haven't truly spoken to you in ten years, after all. But I'll understand if you don't wish to stay."

How could he respond to that without making it seem that he didn't care? "I'll stay," he said. "For a little while. And then I'll check on Enapay, and she can keep you company."

"I'd like that," Skade murmured, but her eyes closed before she could utter another word. For a moment, Michael froze, expecting death, or worse, but her breathing was steady and color now tinted her cheeks. She had exhausted herself, that was all.

And that was enough. With a mind to his promise, Michael sat with her, uncomplaining. He had nothing left to complain about, after all, now that one of his dearest wishes had come true.

Chapter 15

Alban opened his eyes. For a moment, he could not remember what had happened, or how he came to be in such simple surroundings with a colorful quilt covering his body and warming his soul. He felt the shreds of his father's spell deep inside his mind, but they were dead things, no longer a threat to his sanity.

Just for the novelty, he curled one hand into a fist and felt his fingernails dimple his skin. He saw no chains; in fact, no *mark* of the chains that had imprisoned him, but that did not mean he was free.

Although...didn't he remember something about a dark-skinned woman with kind eyes and a ready smile whose hands glowed with an amber light? His mind supplied her name--Espen--and then coughed up everything else.

Or, nearly everything else. There were things that even his mind did not want to examine.

He had been a prisoner, again. Something had happened; something horrible, and he had been locked away in a tiny cage and left to starve while his father milked his innate powers for all they were worth. He had been rescued...by the vampire.

His brother. Yes. That felt right.

Alban glanced into the shadows that surrounded his bed, and found the familiar figure of his brother asleep in a chair covered with thickly stuffed upholstery. In the dim glow of a lamp, his brother looked both thin and pale, as if he had not left Alban's side at all.

He wondered what would happen now that he was awake. Were they safe in Espen's house or would Terrin find a way to steal them back again?

He shifted position, half-expecting to feel the aches and pains of healing wounds, but everything seemed to be intact. Except for the nagging feeling that he had missed something important, he felt perfectly fine.

"Before you try to get up, I have to tell you something important," the vampire whispered from the darkness of his chair.

Alban would have jumped, but he had sensed a split second before Alexander began to speak that he was awake. "What?" his voice cracked. "You...you freed me, didn't you?"

"I helped you free yourself," the vampire said. "And...I want you to know that he forced me to..."

"To make me into a vampire." Alban guessed the cause of his anguish without any trouble at all. "I know."

The vampire's eyes glittered from the shadows. "You understand I wouldn't have wished this on anyone?"

"I understand." Alban managed a small smile. "But...thank you."

"For what?" the vampire's voice cracked, and Alban realized he was crying.

"For saving my life, of course," he said.

Although the thought as to what would have happened if the vampire had refused would not be banished from his mind. His father wouldn't have been able to hold him, and he certainly wouldn't have been able to...Alban frowned. He had no memories, in truth, but he knew something bad had happened.

When Terrin was involved, something bad always happened.

"What happened?" he asked. "While I was...unconscious."

The vampire leaned forward, his tears momentarily forgotten. "What do you remember?"

Alban shivered. "Dying, I think. And...I remember the spell. And Terrin told you your name."

"Yes. It still doesn't *feel* like my name, though."

"Did you...have any of your powers returned?"

"I haven't begun to Dream, if that's what you want to know," the vampire said. "I'm hoping...I hope it never returns."

"I wish..." Alban sighed. "This never would have happened if I wasn't a wizard."

"That's true," the vampire said, "but I can no more change the past than you can. Hopefully now, at least, someone will be able to teach you to hold Terrin at bay if he tries to trap you again."

Hopefully. Alban didn't like the sound of that, but he had no cause for complaint. There hadn't been *enough* time, before. Now, *hopefully*, there would be plenty of time for training.

"What happened in Leysan?" he asked again. "Is everyone okay?" *Is everyone alive?* He dared not ask the question he wanted to ask.

The vampire sighed. "Yes and no. Alive, yes. Okay...no."

The steady drone of his voice as he recounted what had happened almost cast Alban back into darkness again, but he managed to stay awake for most of the story.

What he remembered colored his dreams.

Chapter 16

Terrin could not believe his luck. He had not expected to find Nicodemus alive, or Kyne, and he wondered how he could make best of this unexpected opportunity. He had no doubt he could ransom his son for Nicodemus, if he phrased his demand correctly, but what could he do about Kyne? He did not want to court the wrath of Severin's Queen. He had come too close to her wrath before.

His plans lay in shambles, but he thought he might be able to salvage his kingdom. And perhaps, if he played his cards right, he would claim both Leysan and Glinyeu and begin to expand his empire.

He left his new prisoners alone for the time being, and concentrated on the preparation of his spell. To infect so many at once took careful planning. To make sure his spell was strong enough to kill them all took a bit more than that. He would succeed if he killed a few at a time, but he didn't want his guards--of which there were far too few--to have to quell a stampede when they realized what he planned.

As far as they were concerned, so far, he had detained them to find a gang of thieves.

He stared out at the milling detainees, picking out the ones most likely to have power. At a silent signal, the guards closed and locked every one of the doors. Not many of his victims noticed. Terrin breathed life into his spell, linking it with the brief lives of the castle spiders. Silently, they scurried down the walls towards their prey.

He watched as the ones closest to the walls were bitten, until a veritable sea of people below him writhed in pain from the deadly bite of his spell. As quickly as he dared, Terrin drew off their power, replenishing his depleted stores.

For some reason, power drawn from the dead and dying tasted sweeter than power drawn from despair. As these nameless travelers writhed on the floor beneath him, he drank their deaths until he could drink no more.

Unfortunately, he could not arbitrarily murder anyone without eventual repercussions. That was why he needed to win his son back from Espen.

And now he had enough power to make that attempt.

Chapter 17

The Dream began almost before Zaira closed her eyes; an impending sense of doom had dogged her steps all evening.

She saw Espen's house, lying so still in the middle of a vast forest, and the garden that grew around it. The kitchen window glowed softly on the lilacs outside, but there was no other sign of life.

For a moment, in her Dream, she stood there, uncertain, not understanding the meaning of what she saw.

A shadow flickered on the other side of the window, but she could not make out its identity. Zaira glanced around her at the silent garden, waiting for inspiration to strike, but nothing happened.

After a little while, she walked down the stone path until she could see into the kitchen window. But instead of death or destruction, she merely saw herself, sitting at Espen's kitchen table with a mug of tea in one hand.

Teluride sat at the opposite end of the table, his eyes shadowed, but she felt a bit strengthened to know he would be able to make it as far as the kitchen someday soon. She watched the cozy scene for a little while until her

Dream eyes grew heavy, and then turned from the window. *Why* had she Dreamed this? What warning did this Dream hold?

A movement in the window caught her eye, and she stared out at her own face, so different now, seeing it not as a reflection but as another person would have seen it. The expression in this other Zaira's eyes gave her pause, for it bordered on ferocity she *knew* she did not possess.

Why had she Dreamed this? What was wrong?

Behind her double, Teluride's head lowered to the table, as if the sheer strength it took for him to walk into the kitchen and drink a cup of tea had overcome him at last. Her double turned and smiled.

And Zaira watched in horror as her double--her*self*!--drew out a shiny dagger, crossed the room to where Teluride sat, and calmly drew the blade across his neck.

Zaira stepped away from the window. Her hands flew up to her throat as bright blood spilled across the table. Teluride didn't twitch, or awaken.

The true horror of what she had Dreamed made the scene in front of her shimmer and begin to fade. Zaira let it fade, unable to comprehend what she had seen.

How could *she* so calmly murder Teluride? How could she drug him and then murder him? She stared down at her hands and tried to imagine picking up a dagger and drawing it across someone's throat. *Teluride's* throat. She could not conceive that she would do such a thing.

But her Dreams had never lied before.

Her Dreams had *never* lied before.

The Dream dissolved and she awoke in her now-familiar bed, barely able to see Espen's colorful quilts through the tears in her eyes. Zaira wiped them away, unable to forget the horrible thing she had seen; the horrible thing she would do.

But how? How could she do such a thing?

She realized *how* didn't matter anymore. What mattered was that this terrible thing would happen if she didn't find a way to stop it.

And the only way she could think of to stop it was to leave. Leave Espen's familiar house and venture out into the wilds of the forest and try not to allow Terrin to find her.

Almost without realizing it, she made a mental list of her possessions-- dreadfully few. She would take clothes, but not everything Espen had given her. She would take food, but only a small amount.

She had survived on so little for six years, after all. Surely she could survive on a small amount for a little longer. At least not until after the crisis had passed and she Dreamed Teluride alive and healthy again.

A peek out the window showed it was close to dawn; a fine enough time to leave. Zaira slipped on her clothes and packed a few things in a handy bag. Then she eased open her door and walked down the hall.

Teluride's door opened as she approached. Zaira tensed; sure that he would discover her, but he did not appear in the doorway.

Why, then, had the door opened?

Curious now, she set her bag outside the door and opened it the rest of the way. Teluride lay in bed, asleep, but when she approached, he opened his eyes.

Zaira stepped back, but she knew her Dream would not come true for a little while. Teluride didn't have enough strength to walk to the kitchen yet, after all. But still, she could not stay around knowing that she would murder him sometime in the future.

"I couldn't sleep," Teluride whispered. "I'm sorry; did I wake you?"

Zaira bit her lip. "No. But I saw your door open, and I thought..." What did she think? That he would catch her as she left? He wouldn't be able to catch anyone. He barely had enough strength to eat. "I just wanted to make sure you were okay."

Teluride smiled. "Thank you. I think I had a bad dream, but I know it was a dream now."

"What did you dream about?" Zaira asked curiously.

Something shimmered in Teluride's gaze, almost as if he had dreamed of the same horrible thing as Zaira had. She wondered if he had, but she didn't dare ask.

"It was nothing," Teluride whispered. "An old dream. A terrible memory." He shrugged. "Where are you going?"

It was a direct question, and Zaira couldn't lie to him. She cursed the feeling that had made her check on him one last time.

She licked her lips. "I'm going away."

"Away?" Teluride frowned, not understanding. "What do you mean?"

"Away. I have to leave." She could not couch the words in anything but the truth. "I...I dreamed something horrible and now I have to leave."

"Leave Espen's house?" Teluride stared at her. "But won't Terrin..."

"I'll make sure Terrin doesn't find me," Zaira said before he could finish the question. She had no idea *how* she could hide herself from Terrin, but she intended to try.

Teluride was silent for the longest time. Zaira couldn't decide whether he wanted to talk her out of it or wish her luck. She couldn't decide which way she would prefer. Certainly, she couldn't stay in Espen's house, knowing what she knew. But could she tell someone--anyone--and have *them* make the decision for her?

"I'm very sorry you feel you have to leave," Teluride whispered. "I'll miss you, Zaira."

Zaira's eyes filled with tears again. "I'll miss you too. But this is the only way to stop what I Dreamed." She could say that, even if she did not know it was true.

And before she could lose her nerve, she turned her back on Teluride and left.

No one met her in the hall, and no one stopped her as she slipped outside. She allowed herself to look back once, just before Espen's house vanished into the trees, and then she faced the rising sun.

To save Teluride's life, she would do this, and she would not regret her decision.

Chapter 18

"What will come..."

Kyne awoke to the sound of Nicodemus' voice, hoarse and faint in the darkness.

"What will come is almost too horrible to contemplate."

She couldn't tell if he spoke in his sleep, or to whom he directed this enigmatic phrase of words.

"What *will come,* Nicodemus?"

At first, she thought he would not answer. He lay in silence for a long time, and then he spoke.

"Death. Destruction."

"Whose death?" Kyne sat up and peered into the darkness, straining to see his face.

Nicodemus started to reply, but something--his Dream, perhaps--caught in his throat. He choked, coughed, and Kyne saw his shadowy form sit up and lean against the wall. "What did I say?"

She saw him clearly enough to watch him rub his throat, but she couldn't see the expression on his face.

"'That you saw death and destruction in the future," Kyne replied. "Do you remember what you Dreamed?"

"Yes, but..." He raised one shaking hand, then lowered it. "I...I feel...strange."

Kyne crossed the room to where he sat. "Is it Terrin's spell?" Without a light, she couldn't see the spell's influence in his gaze or judge the paleness of his skin.

"Not...not exactly." He passed one hand across his face. His other hand sought her arm and squeezed. "It's...I can't feel it anymore."

"It's almost dawn," Kyne said. "I should be able to tell if the spell is gone." She waited beside him until the little room was light enough, then searched his gaze for the familiar taint of Terrin's spell. His eyes were full of anguish and pain, but she neither sensed nor saw the spell lurking anywhere in his body.

"I feel..." He lowered his head to his hands and his filthy hair hid his lost expression. "What will he do now that I'm not dead?"

"I'm not sure," Kyne said. "Does it still hurt if someone asks you a question?"

"I don't know," Nicodemus whispered. "I'm not...ask me a question."

"How can we escape and get to Espen's house before Cathan strikes?" Kyne asked.

Nicodemus tensed, but when nothing happened, the tension slowly leaked out of his bearing. "Soon," he said, and Kyne had the feeling he was leaving out some of the truth. "It won't be long now..." He raised his head and met Kyne's gaze. "I'm cured, aren't I?" He did not sound very happy about that fact.

"I think you are," Kyne said. "How do you feel?"

"Weak. And hungry." He said this as if the admission surprised him. "Thank you for everything you've done for me, Kyne. I will owe you my life."

His curious phrasing piqued her interest, but she had no time to call him on it. A key turned in the lock, and the heavy oak door slowly opened.

Terrin had returned.

Chapter 19

When Cathan awoke, his first thought was to make sure his ruse had worked and Espen hadn't discovered his identity. Finding that he lay in a bed and not a dungeon helped strengthen his hope that he had succeeded, and when he slipped out of bed and discovered that the door to his room wasn't locked, he knew he had fooled the most powerful Healer in the whole of Cruinne.

He stared at Nicodemus' face in the mirror, and tried to plot his course of action. *Staying* Nicodemus would not be difficult, but if he wanted to strengthen Terrin's claim to the throne, he had to pick another persona to achieve his true agenda.

Who would be the last person Espen would believe to be a murderer? Cathan sat down on his bed and picked at one of the witch's damnable quilts. As far as he knew, only Terrin's sons, Teluride, and the Prophet hid in Espen's house with Skade and her son. Cathan would dearly love to pin everything on Michael again, but he wanted to be a bit more creative this time.

If he planned to kill Teluride, then who would the prince trust? Cathan doubted Teluride and Michael had had a chance to meet, and he didn't want to blame anything on Terrin's sons. Terrin himself would take care of them.

That left Skade or Zaira, and the Iomarian Queen had been infected with Terrin's spell. She wouldn't be strong enough to lure Teluride out of his room...but Zaira could.

Cathan sat for a moment and thought about what he knew of the little girl. To make it work, he'd have to ensure Zaira vanished after Teluride's death, and that probably meant he would have to kill her as well. Which would be no great strain, in truth.

His eyes were drawn to the mirror that hung on the far wall, glowing dimly in the predawn light. *Did he* dare *contact Terrin now?* If he succeeded, he would need a quick avenue of escape, and Terrin would have to be poised to strike.

Silently, so as not to set off any of Espen's wards, he stroked the surface of the mirror and examined it for spells. Espen's protections were simple to get past now that he stood *inside* her spells, but he also did not want to leave a trace behind that the witch could track.

He could not make a portal, of course, but Terrin could. Cathan only had enough power to contact him and tell him of his plan.

With exquisite care, he eased past Espen's visible spells and whispered the spell that would show him where Terrin had fled. The mirror shimmered, and then abruptly shifted to show a small, sparsely furnished room in Glinyeu. Terrin was not evident, but an unmade bed showed Cathan that the room was, at least, occupied.

He would wait, then, and listen for Espen's footsteps. That would give Terrin enough time to return to his room, and Cathan enough time to finish thinking through his plan.

With his plan in place, he only had to wait until it was time to strike.

And then, Terrin would get his sons back and strike a fatal blow into the heart of Espen's stronghold.

Chapter 20

Zaira did not want to leave; she had to leave. At least that's what she tried to tell herself as she walked through the forest, careful to stay away from any paths, even those obviously made by deer.

She had no doubt Espen had unannounced visitors all the time, even though she had yet to see anyone who did not fit in. Still, it would not hurt to make sure she was not seen.

So, she kept to the least civilized portions of the forest, fighting through brush and wild roses until she reached a broad stream.

She had not missed her life in the tower until now.

Trapped in the tower, she had been content to pretend that the people she saw in her Dreams were not real; that the death and destruction was only a figment of her imagination, even though she knew it was not.

But meeting Skade, Teluride, the vampire, and Alban, not to mention Skade's son, Michael, and his little daughter Enapay, brought home the reality of her Dreams and left her heart aching at what she saw. What she Dreamed she would do, even though she could not--in any way--believe that she was capable of such a thing.

Hot tears flooded her eyes. Why couldn't she have had a little while longer to enjoy Espen's home? How could she so calmly murder Teluride without losing her mind--or worse? She could not imagine that she could do such a thing, and yet...and yet she had Dreamed it, and everyone knew Dreams did not lie.

Zaira was so wrapped up in her own misery that she didn't notice the small figure following her. She probably wouldn't have noticed Enapay at all if the little girl had not stepped in a hole, fallen, and cried out.

"Enapay?" Zaira turned, her heart suddenly cold in her chest. She had not foreseen this; in fact, she had Dreamed nothing about Michael's daughter at all. In fact, she didn't even know anything about what happened to the others...perhaps she would kill them all. Who was she to wonder? A murderer could kill anyone, after all. She had tried to change the course, but perhaps she'd now kill Enapay instead!

Enapay rose, tottered a little, and dusted off her dress. "Why are you leaving?"

Zaira stared at her. "You should go back."

"I can't. I followed you," Enapay pointed out. "I wanted to find out why you're running away."

"Why do you think I'm running away?" Thankfully, Zaira had not stolen any weapons, so she knew she wouldn't be able to slit Enapay's throat as easily as she had Dreamed she slit Teluride's throat. But there were other ways to kill someone, she thought. Drowning, a horrible fall...she backed away as Enapay approached.

"You don't seem to be very happy about it, and you only told Teluride you were leaving," Enapay said with impeccable logic. "I don't want you to leave, Zaira."

She looked so...young standing there, her dress all covered with leaves. So innocent. Again, Zaira could not imagine murdering her...or anyone.

"I don't want to leave," Zaira admitted. "But I *have* to leave. You..." Oh, how she wanted to tell someone what she had Dreamed. "You wouldn't understand."

"I'm not a baby," Enapay said crossly.

Zaira felt her lips curve up into a smile. "I know."

"If you don't want to leave, then why do you have to?" Enapay pressed, refusing to give up.

"Because I Dreamed something horrible," Zaira whispered, staring out across the stream. "Something I can't allow to happen."

A small hand touched her arm. "My Mommy told my Daddy that if you talk about horrible things they aren't so horrible anymore."

"Did he take her advice?" Zaira already knew what horrible things Michael didn't want to talk about, but they were nothing compared to her own personal horrible thing.

Enapay giggled. "I don't think so. At least not around me."

What would it hurt to tell her? Zaira didn't want Enapay to run away and hurt herself or get lost, just because of one horrible Dream. "I...I Dreamed something that I can't believe will happen," she whispered.

"Then it won't happen," Enapay said.

Zaira's eyes filled with tears. "My Dreams *always* come true. You don't understand."

Enapay wrapped her arms around Zaira's shoulders and hugged her tight. "Don't cry, Zaira."

Zaira wiped her eyes. "I can't help it. I...I wish I'd never left the tower, Enapay. I wouldn't mind so much, if I hadn't been free."

"Don't say that," Enapay whispered, "we couldn't be friends if you weren't free."

This was true, but Zaira couldn't release the thought that what was to come would have been easier for her to bear if she were still Terrin's prisoner. "You don't understand. You can't understand."

"What did you see?" Enapay asked, as if she had just realized the import of Zaira's words. She stepped away from Zaira and looked back the way they had come, as if straining for a glimpse of Espen's cottage.

"I saw..." Zaira started to describe what she had seen, then remembered Enapay was only six and still a child. "I...I saw myself murder Teluride." She could not meet Enapay's gaze to see the horror on her face, but Zaira knew it would be there.

"I don't believe it," Enapay said after a moment. "You couldn't kill anybody."

"I didn't think so either, but my Dreams don't lie," Zaira said. "That's why I left."

Enapay solemnly stared at the silent forest. "Where are you going to go?"

Zaira sighed. "I don't know." She had left in such a hurry that she hadn't thought much about where she would end up. "I...I didn't want to hurt Teluride, Enapay."

Enapay froze, as if struck by a horrible thought. "How far into the future did you see?"

Zaira closed her eyes and tried to picture the horrible scene in her mind. She had stood outside Espen's window, and the plants had looked the same. But Enapay had asked her a question. Shouldn't she *know* the answer, just like that? "Ask me again," she commanded, opening her eyes.

"How far into the future did you see?" Enapay obeyed without a single hesitation.

Nothing happened. No answer, no vision, no Dream. Zaira's hands rose to her mouth of their own accord. Which meant... Which *usually* meant that it had already happened. But how could it have already happened? She had not murdered him before she fled...

Had she?

"Ask me what will happen to Teluride," she whispered, numb.

"What will happen to Teluride?" Enapay asked.

Again, the same Dream; the same resolution. Only this time... This time, Zaira stared into the eyes of her double and saw a stranger.

Her throat was almost too dry to force out the words. "Enapay, ask me about Nicodemus. Ask me where he is."

"I liked Nicodemus," Enapay said. "I miss him."

"I miss him too," Zaira admitted. "And I thought..." She shivered, imagining what would happen if what she suspected were true. "Ask me, Enapay."

"Where is Nicodemus?" Enapay asked.

Zaira's blood ran cold when the Dream rose up in her mind--of Nicodemus alive again and locked in a tower with Kyne for company. She had no way to contact him, but he *was* alive, and definitely *not* lying in a bed inside the sanctuary of Espen's house.

"We have to go back," she whispered. "We have to *hurry*." She grabbed Enapay's hand.

"What's wrong?" Enapay asked. "What did you see?"

Zaira thought about her Dream and realized how perfect Cathan's scheme truly was. She would have gone her merry way, never realizing that she was the only one who could *stop* Teluride's untimely death. "The person Espen and I rescued from the forest isn't Nicodemus," she said as she hurried through the brush. "It's Cathan."

Enapay stopped cold. "Cathan! He...he...he tried to be my Daddy!"

"And he's going to kill Teluride if we don't hurry up," Zaira said, praying she could remember the way back to Espen's cottage.

This time, Enapay outdistanced Zaira. And they ran to stop a murderer...before it was too late

Chapter 21

Two pale guards preceded Terrin. Kyne remembered the people in the hall and wondered how the guards could have stood there and watched them die. The two men seemed a bit shaken, but little more.

Terrin, on the other hand, seethed with stolen power. Kyne wouldn't have been surprised to see a glowing rainbow in his wake.

Nicodemus struggled to sit up. Kyne didn't dare turn her head to look at him, but she could feel the strength of his tension even without catching his gaze. She wished he had been more forthcoming about what would happen next, though. She would have been very happy to trust in a plan instead of chance.

"Nicodemus."

Out of the corner of her eye, Kyne saw Nicodemus lick his lips. "Terrin."

"You didn't die."

"Not yet," Nicodemus whispered. "What do you want?"

"I've come for your answer," Terrin said. The two guards now flanked him, as if they expected an attack instead of a conversation. "Will you join me, Nicodemus?"

"You know I won't." Nicodemus needed no vision to answer *that* question.

"I was afraid you wouldn't," Terrin said, and he actually sounded sorry about it. "But you see, in truth, I have no need of your loyalty to use your talent."

"I know." Nicodemus stood, leaning against the wall for support.

Bewildered, Kyne scrambled to her feet. "What did you see, Nicodemus?" She stepped in front of him when he avoided her gaze, ignoring Terrin for the time being. "What did you see?"

Nicodemus stared at her, his eyes filled with tears. "I...enjoyed living, at least for a little while," he whispered. "And I'll try to return. Don't let Terrin bury me, Kyne."

A heartbeat later, he collapsed in her arms. Terrin pushed her away and tore Nicodemus from her grasp. Kyne moved back, half-tempted to flee, but she didn't want to leave Nicodemus with Terrin, even though he... She stared at his slack face. What had he told her, back in Leysan? How had he explained it?

"A piece of me...of my spirit...is trapped in a crystal Cathan carries with him. I will be able to track him."

Not only track him, Kyne thought. He'd had the means to escape all along. But would he be able to return to his body, or had he given up his life for his Queen? *Could* he warn them, trapped in a crystal?

"What did you do to him?" Terrin hissed, spinning from his crouch so quickly that Kyne barely saw him move. "What sorcery did you cast?"

Kyne tried to keep her voice calm. "I don't know. He refused to tell me what he saw."

"You lie." Terrin raised his hand and it filled with a glow so intense Kyne had to look away.

"Why would I lie?" she asked. "I have no reason not to tell you the truth. If you recall, Severin is *not* at war with Leysan."

"But you would not support my bid for the throne," Terrin snapped. "And you know too much as it is. Did your sister send you here?"

"I told you the truth before," Kyne said, watching the glowing ball of light in Terrin's hand out of the corner of her eye. She had no magic to combat something like that, not without plenty of preparation. "I came to Leysan to discover what had happened, and found the castle nearly empty. When I found Nicodemus, he was half out of his mind from the pain. I thought I would take him to a Healer, but your guards found us first." She paused. "I truly have no idea what is going on. Just what my sister told me, and even that wasn't much."

Terrin tested her words and found them true enough. He scowled. "And what did your sister tell you?"

Kyne shrugged. "That something had happened in Leysan, but she didn't know what. It was my job to report back to her if I discovered what had happened."

"What happened was that Skade and her friends decided to make my business their own," Terrin snarled. "They stole my sons and my prisoners and left me with nothing."

"Your *sons*?" The words slipped out before Kyne could stop herself.

Terrin scowled, as if he truly wanted to launch the glowing spell at Kyne and stop her questions once and for all, but he showed extraordinary restraint--for Terrin. "What will you report to your sister?"

Kyne's heart lurched. *Did he intend to just let her go? But what about Nicodemus?*

She chose her words with care. "That I went to Leysan and found one survivor, but he never regained consciousness long enough to tell me what happened." She truly doubted he would accept that explanation or believe she wouldn't fill in the details of whom she had found.

Terrin glanced back at Nicodemus' body. "Did you tell your sister everything my son did to you?"

Only because she expected him to ask a similar question was Kyne able to keep her voice and expression neutral. Inside, she seethed. She had no recourse of action against a true wizard, save trying to escape with her skin intact. "Of course not." Against her better judgment, she allowed her anger to show, just a little.

"I doubted you would." Terrin motioned to the guards. "Bring him and leave her here."

Kyne stepped forward. "What are you going to do to him?"

"I'm half-tempted to burn his body, if he is truly dead, but I want to find out what happened first..." He would have said more, Kyne thought, but something invisible caught his attention. Something strange enough for the masks to slip and show her the madness that now ruled Terrin's mind. "What..." He whispered that and another word Kyne didn't catch, and nearly ran from the room.

The two guards looked at each other, then at Kyne. "Your king could be under attack," she suggested, and backed her words with what little suggestive power she held.

Surprisingly, it worked. The guards rushed after Terrin, leaving her alone with Nicodemus' body and facing an open door. Kyne shook her head. They would never learn.

"Nicodemus?" On the off chance he had tricked Terrin into thinking he was dead, Kyne spoke his name. Nothing happened. His skin was already cool to the touch; his chest still. She wondered if he would be able to return.

He would not *want* to live again if his Queen died by Cathan's hand. Kyne knew that just from their conversations. Skade might have raped his mind as Terrin claimed, but she had created such loyalty...and didn't Nicodemus' loyalty deserve a just reward?

Kyne bit her lip. She wouldn't be able to escape with Nicodemus' body in tow. A dead weight was one thing, but a body... And there were no hiding places in this little room, at least.

In the end, she dragged him down the hall and stashed him in an unused bedroom that housed a single bed, a battered table, and a mirror on the wall, just in case.

Chapter 22

Cathan was just about to break the connection when Terrin opened the door in Leysan and scowled at the mirror.

The expression on his face immediately changed when he saw Cathan's face in the mirror.

Cathan forced a smile. "You left me for dead."

For a moment, Terrin just stared. And then, slowly, he began to smile. "Cathan."

Cathan bowed. "In the flesh. I'm standing in Espen's cottage, Terrin, and they don't suspect a thing." He decided to hold mention of trapping Nicodemus' spirit in the crystal, just in case things did not work out as planned. After all, he *could* use Nicodemus as a hostage if he needed to.

"Until she catches you using her mirror," Terrin snapped.

"I used precautions. I'm not as stupid as you think."

For a moment, Cathan thought Terrin would disagree, but he accepted Cathan's forward thinking with a sour nod. "You did well. What do you plan to do?"

"I thought I might relieve some of your burden by killing your nephew," Cathan said. "With Teluride's death, the kingdom would rightfully be yours."

"True," Terrin said, "but I already hold the kingdom. Teluride's continued health is of no concern to me. If you truly wish to kill him, then proceed."

"Good. I'd already decided to kill him as Zaira; she's the only one he might trust. And then, I thought I might kill Skade as well..."

"She's still alive?" Terrin shook his head. "She should be dead. Are you certain she's still alive?"

Cathan stepped back from the mirror even though he knew Terrin could not strike him through it without opening a portal. "N...no, but I assumed..."

"Assume nothing where the Queen of Iomar is concerned," Terrin said. "Find out if she lives and kill her. I want *her* dead more than my nephew."

"But why?" Cathan dared to ask.

"Because her presence keeps me from my ultimate goal," Terrin said. "Kill her, and I will give you a kingdom of your own to rule, Cathan. I swear I will."

The stakes had just been raised. Cathan had to swallow twice to wet his throat. "A...a kingdom?"

"Glinyeu is in need of a King, as is Aberdus," Terrin said. "I will see to it that you are on the throne of either kingdom."

A throne. His own kingdom. Somehow, the risks involved with assuring Skade's death paled in comparison.

"Consider it done," he said.

"Good." Terrin glanced back over his shoulder, as if he expected someone to appear. "I have some...unfinished business to attend to here, but I will be outside Espen's lair in a couple of hours. I trust there's a stream or such nearby that will hold a portal?"

"There's a creek not far away from the cottage," Cathan said, his heart pounding.

"Good. If you can, distract the witch enough for me to slip through her wards."

"Consider it done," Cathan said again. For the reward of a kingdom, he would make sure it was.

Chapter 23

Michael left Skade asleep in her bed and quietly let himself out of her room. It was after dawn now, and sunlight streamed through the closest windows, but the rest of Espen's house was in shadow.

He knew he should go back to his room and sleep, but he knew he would just toss and turn until the rest of the household awoke. He should contact Lucas, and assure him all was, if not well, then bearable for the time being. He should...

He should do a lot of things, but exhaustion would not serve him well for doing any of it. Still, Michael hesitated outside of Enapay's door before he entered his own room, then decided that one last glimpse of his sleeping daughter would do before he tried to get some rest.

Michael didn't realize her bed was empty until he sat down on the rickety wooden chair and saw that the rumpled bedclothes held nothing but air.

For a moment, all he could do was sit there and stare at her empty bed in shock. His first thought--after the denial that she was really gone--was to look for a mirror in the room. He would not put it past Terrin to kidnap her again for some ungodly reason.

But Enapay's room was one of the few *without* a mirror. And a moment after he expected the worst, Michael realized her absence might have a purely mundane reason.

She *was* only six years old, after all. And Michael knew from experience that six-year-old children had very small bladders.

He didn't remember rising from the chair and rushing from her room. He slowed down right outside the kitchen doorway, fixing the scene he hoped to see in his mind. Enapay sitting at the table, drinking hot chocolate with Espen.

But the kitchen was empty and cold. And when he peeked into the bathroom, it was empty as well.

The fear that she was gone--never too far away to begin with--returned full-force. Michael's knees almost gave out. He clutched the back of one of Espen's chairs and tried to breathe deeply enough to wash away the fear. There could still be a mundane reason for her absence. Perhaps she had decided to visit one of Espen's other guests. Michael had not been in his room, and he doubted Enapay knew where to find Skade's room.

Michael had yet to meet any of the others. He'd expected Espen to introduce him to everyone eventually, but she had yet to broach the subject. He knew who they were, of course. But which one would Enapay have visited enough to feel comfortable with? Michael had no idea.

He would have to at least peek in every room to find her. Michael closed his eyes, sent up a silent prayer to whatever deity might be watching over his daughter, and left the kitchen.

He did not notice that the front door to Espen's cottage was cracked just enough to let in a spill of dawn sunlight.

Chapter 24

Long after Alban fell asleep, the vampire sat and watched his brother, his mind sluggish now that the immediate threat of Terrin was further away.

He felt as if he had lived on the edge of a precipice for many years, and that the precipice had crumbled, launching him into the unknown. He had no idea what the future held; or if he *had* a future. Terrin had held sway over his mind and body for so long that even this small amount of freedom left him blinking in dazed amazement at what he had been missing.

After a while, he must have slipped off to sleep, because Alban no longer lay in the bed next to his chair. Instead, he saw a woman with red hair--not Skade, but someone else--all dressed in white. And beside her bed, another one, and another one, and another.

Somehow, he had returned to the room beneath Leysan's castle he had found after he escaped.

What had Espen called them? *The Sleepers.* Yes. But why dream of them now?

And why dream at all? He couldn't remember the last time he had truly Dreamed. Why now? He took a step forward, then glanced over his shoulder to make sure the mirror still leaned against the wall. At least then, if this were not a Dream, but real, he could escape again.

The Sleepers slept on. The vampire made a slow circuit of the room, then faced the mirror as he had before. His reflection rippled in the mirror's glass.

Why was he here?

He heard a shifting sound behind him, but nothing showed in the reflection of the mirror. Half-expecting to see Terrin appear amid the Sleepers, he turned.

The red-haired woman in the third bed on his left had changed. Before, she had merely resembled Skade in skin tone and hair color. But now...now, she had turned into the Iomarian Queen in all her resplendent beauty.

The vampire abandoned the mirror and approached Skade's bed, wondering if this truly *was* a glimpse of what the future would bring. Would Skade end up with the Sleepers, neither dead nor alive?

As soon as he stopped by the side of her bed, she opened her eyes. For a moment, she did not speak, and then she smiled at him, a smile so full of beauty that the vampire felt his eyes fill with tears.

"Do you know why you're here, Alexander?" Her voice cracked.

He had not realized Skade knew his name. "No. I don't." He fumbled for the words he wanted to speak, but could not force them past the lump in his throat. "I don't want you to die," he said instead, but it was a faint shadow of his true feelings.

"There is a way you can save us," Skade said. "A way to save *all* of us."

"How?" He thought he would do anything--even give up his life--to save hers. "What must I do?"

Now he knew why her subjects and slaves held such loyalty for her. They were all secretly in love with their Queen...Nicodemus, her servants, her maids...and the vampire himself.

"You hold the key to the antidote to Terrin's spell," Skade said.

The vampire stepped back. "How? I don't understand."

"Nicodemus told me how to cure Terrin's spell--and how to stop Terrin--but he did not understand his Dream." Skade's eyes glittered with tears. "Now that he is gone...now that he is gone, he will never understand. But I can. And you will. What do you see?"

The vampire looked around, struggling to find meaning in the dream. "I see the Sleepers," he whispered. "At least that's what Espen called them."

"They are under a stasis spell that does not advance the symptoms of Terrin's spell," Skade said. "It was the only thing we could do for them. There is another room like this in Iomar, but it's twice this size." She was silent for a long moment. "Once...once, I thought my own son would die in a room like this."

"Michael was infected?" the vampire asked. Somehow, this seemed important, because if Michael had been infected, he had survived.

And how had he survived?

"I thought he was," Skade said. "But it turned out to be guilt instead of Terrin's spell. Guilt."

The vampire knew as well as anyone that guilt could have disastrous effects on a person's health, but he didn't say that out loud. Skade's tone of voice held no argument; only fact.

A movement behind him made him look at his reflection in the mirror again, but this time, part of his face was marred by a drying streak of blood--the same streak of blood he had smeared across the mirror in the hope to contact Skade before. The streak of blood that hadn't been on the mirror mere minutes ago. The vampire could not tear his gaze away from it.

"What do you see?" Skade asked again, her voice fainter now, as if Terrin's spell had sapped the rest of her strength.

"I see...blood," he whispered.

The word struck a chord inside his heart, as if *blood* held more than just sustenance. The vampire left Skade's side and drifted towards the mirror, still unable to look away.

When he reached it and touched the smear of blood on the cold glass, he found it still wet to the touch. Still wet. Without thinking, he raised his wet fingers to his lips. A cacophony of images struck his mind, in no apparent order.

Terrin, standing over a table full of glass bottles and jars, his teeth clenched as he drew a small dagger across his wrist.

The hiss of contact as his blood spilled into a murky potion.

The mumbled words he spoke to finish it; his triumph, his spell.

The vampire *almost* understood.

He touched the mirror and it shimmered into life, projecting what he saw onto its surface.

Terrin, standing over a table full of glass bottles and jars, his teeth clenched as he drew a small dagger across his wrist.

Blood. Blood.

In the end, it all came down to blood, didn't it?

And then, he knew, just like that. Knew with a certainty that echoed when he had Dreamed for Terrin...that blood *was* the answer. Not Terrin's blood, not the maker of the spell, even though his blood was inexorably tied to his creation.

No, not Terrin's blood, although the vampire thought Terrin's blood might help the afflicted. But there was one person who had survived the spell--and one person, now dead, who might have survived.

Zaira. And Nicodemus. Both Dreamers. Zaira had survived, but the spell had changed her. The vampire didn't know if Nicodemus would have survived, but since Zaira had, the vampire thought he might have eventually recovered his strength.

But Terrin had killed him before that could happen.

A potion made from Zaira's blood would cure Skade and the others, but not stop Terrin's madness. There was a way, the vampire *knew* there was a way to stop him, but he couldn't quite...couldn't quite reach past the shadows blocking the answer from his mind.

Did he already know the answer? He could not force it to come if he did, but he could attempt to dream again.

Even though he would prefer to stay Dreamless for the rest of his life, he could try. If only to find a way to stop Terrin for good, so he and Alban could be free.

The dreamscape shimmered; the mirror dimmed. The vampire heard a noise that had no basis in the little room; an unfamiliar voice whispering his name.

He turned, half-expecting to see Skade again, but the red-haired woman had returned to her bed, her eyes closed, her face grave. And not one of the Sleepers moved, save for the steady rhythm of their chests.

The voice whispered again. Someone else--Alban, he thought--replied. And then the dream was gone, swirling away into nothingness, leaving him only with a piece of the solution to the whole.

Chapter 25

For a long moment, the pain of Cathan's binding left Nicodemus frozen, unable to explore the constraints of his prison. He missed his body in ways he could not explain; after so long a ghost, sensation was still new to him, and treasured. Even the pain of Terrin's spell was something to cherish.

He opened his eyes to darkness marred only by the faint light of Cathan's binding. It seemed whole from where he stood, but when he drew closer, he realized Cathan had not completely closed the circle. Gaps, where the blood had missed, stained his inner sight, casting great black holes in the binding-- and creating flaws in his crystal prison that had not been in evidence before.

Nicodemus would have rejoiced if he had another place to go, but he knew he had to stay with Cathan long enough to reach Espen's cottage. And even with the gaps in the binding, he could not see outside the velvet bag that covered the crystal and blocked his sight.

He heard muffled voices through the velvet bag, and realized after a moment, that Cathan was speaking to someone. But who? Had he already reached Espen's cottage? He centered his entire being on listening to

Cathan's voice. By the end of the conversation, Nicodemus knew that his time had run out. Cathan had already slipped through Espen's wards. He had already contacted Terrin. And he had a plan to murder Skade, something Nicodemus could not allow to happen.

He struggled with the crystal's binding and felt awareness prickle across his skin as he seeped back through the connection to his body. He did not want to open his eyes to see Terrin's face, but he could not escape the crystal without breaking it...or forcing Cathan to break it himself.

Breath hissed through cold lips. No one raised an alarm. Nicodemus opened his eyes, disoriented by the double vision of the darkened crystal and a bedroom he'd never seen before. He managed to sit up, still expecting Terrin to sound an alarm, and something dim and shadowy moved across the room.

Nicodemus flinched back, then realized that the shadowy figure was himself, and just the reflection in a mirror. A mirror. He almost wept with relief. Whoever had put him here--and it had to be Kyne, hiding him from Terrin while she escaped--had left him with a means of escape himself, if he had enough strength to form a portal.

Nicodemus climbed out of bed and staggered over to the mirror. His vision kept shifting between the crystal hanging around Cathan's neck and the room in Leysan, and he could not force it to stay in one place. Even worse, his fingers and toes alternated between freezing numbness and hyper-awareness, as if he had frostbite or something worse.

He knew he was in no shape to attempt to create a portal, but he also knew he had no true choice. He had to stop Cathan before someone died.

Nicodemus took a deep breath and closed his eyes. He put both hands on the mirror, drawing strength from somewhere deep inside his soul. He had no blood to give to form the portal, so he drew on long experience and formed it from will alone.

Twice, he almost fell into darkness. Twice, his legs weakened and shook, nearly throwing him to the ground. But finally, he managed to create a frail portal between Aberdus' forest and Leysan's castle. Before his strength deserted him, he stepped through it, and plunged into the icy waters of a swiftly flowing stream.

Nicodemus' eyes flew open. He struggled, but his struggles were marred by weakness and utter exhaustion. He swallowed water. Choked. Realized that he could drown and truly die. Tried to see the opposite shore through his tears and when it did not appear, allowed panic to propel him forward.

When he hit the bank, he could not find enough strength to climb through mud and leaves to dry ground. So he clung to a root growing out of the bank and tried to summon up enough strength to drag himself to drier ground.

At first, when he heard voices, he thought he must be hallucinating, for why would Zaira and Enapay be out in the forest? They should be safe in Espen's house. But the voices grew nearer, and soon he heard rustling footsteps that told him they were near.

He could not force his voice above a whisper at first, but panic was again a good catalyst for movement. He raised his head, blinking the mud away, and drew in a deep breath.

"Wait...please..."

The footsteps stopped. Nicodemus became aware of a strong sense of *listening* now, as if the two girls strained to discover his location by sound alone.

"Zaira." He felt blackness press across his vision, but he could not allow it to carry him away. Not yet. "Zaira, please."

Timid footsteps approached. Nicodemus raised his head in time to see Zaira swing a heavy tree branch, almost knocking him into the water again.

"How do I know you're really Nicodemus?" she asked. Behind her, Enapay's fear-pinched face appeared for a brief moment before she, too, lifted a tree branch for defense.

Nicodemus lowered his head to the mud again, too tired to crane his head to look at her. "Because the fake Nicodemus--Cathan--still lies in Espen's cottage, waiting to murder Teluride."

That must have been the right thing to say. This time, instead of trying to brain him with her tree branch, Zaira lowered it so he could pull himself up onto dry ground.

He very nearly did not make it.

Chapter 26

Michael opened the first door and saw a sleeping figure lying in a narrow bed. He did not recognize the young man, but by process of elimination, he realized this was Teluride, the rightful king of Leysan's throne. Enapay was not in his room, watching over him. Since it was doubtful that she'd been in his room at all, Michael let the prince sleep and moved on.

The next room was bare of occupants, the empty bed covered with clothes. Michael guessed this was Zaira's room, but did that make the prophet missing as well? Where could they be?

The next room was Enapay's; the next, Michael's own. He checked both even though he knew they would be empty.

Across the hall were four more rooms. The vampire and Alban remained unaccounted for, and Skade's room was at the very end of the hall. Michael peeked in on his mother, but she had not awakened.

And where was Espen? He had heard no sign of life from the rest of her cottage; no signal that she had not abandoned them to Terrin's whims. As far as he knew the other two rooms would be empty, unless Espen had another patient. Michael couldn't imagine who it could be. Nicodemus was dead, after all, a victim of Terrin's wrath. But he would check both rooms anyway, just in case.

The first room seemed to be an unused bedroom, stark and cold in darkness, the sunlight shuttered away. The second room housed both the vampire and Alban. The latter opened his eyes when Michael peeked inside.

"He's asleep," Alban whispered. "I don't think he's slept since he brought me here."

"I'm looking for Enapay," Michael said, understanding and approving of the vampire's intentions. "Have you seen her? She's not in her bed and I'm getting worried."

"You're her father," Alban whispered. "I remember someone telling me that."

"My name is Michael, and yes, I'm her father."

"I haven't seen her," Alban said. "But you might ask Alexander, when he wakes up."

At the sound of his name, the vampire stirred and opened his eyes. For a moment, Michael thought the vampire did not see him at all, and then a look of pure horror passed over his face.

"Where's Zaira?" He struggled out of his chair. "Where is Zaira?"

Michael's heart froze. "I...she wasn't in her room. I just checked. Enapay is missing too." Should he have sounded an alarm sooner, rather than wasting his time peeking in each and every one of Espen's rooms?

The vampire focused his gaze on Michael, and Michael stepped back. "Who..oh." He shook his head and wiped one hand over his eyes. "You're Skade's son."

"Yes."

"And the little girl...Enapay...is yours."

"Yes. Have you seen her?" Michael couldn't keep the hope out of his voice.

The vampire's gaze softened. "No. I'm sorry, I haven't. But I...I Dreamed, Alban." He turned to his brother. "I Dreamed."

Michael did not know the import of that sentence, but evidently Alban did.

"What did you Dream?" he asked softly, as if afraid the vampire would refuse to answer.

"I saw the cure for Terrin's spell," the vampire said with an anxious glance at Michael. "The blood of one who has survived the spell can be used to make the cure."

"Of one who has survived," Michael repeated. "That's why you asked for Zaira."

"Yes. But if she's missing..."

The full import of what the vampire had said finally sank through the layers of Michael's mind. "You know the cure to Terrin's spell. You know how to save my mother's life."

"Yes." The vampire watched him carefully, as if expecting him to lunge to grab him and force him to tell Espen or Skade what he had Dreamed. "But Nicodemus is dead, and the only other survivor I know of is Zaira."

"Nicodemus isn't dead," Espen said from the hallway, scaring Michael half to death. "Zaira found him right outside my wards early yesterday evening."

Michael turned to face her. "Zaira's not in her room. And neither is Enapay."

The witch seemed to stop breathing. She closed her eyes, and Michael felt her awareness sweep through the cottage, peeking into the many nooks and crannies a child could have strayed upon. After an eternity of waiting, Espen opened her eyes.

"I don't sense Zaira at all," she said, meeting Michael's gaze with her own. "Or Enapay."

Michael fell to his knees. He did not know which way to turn now; Espen's house was no longer safe for anyone.

Espen's hand touched his shoulder.

"Did you steal her to ensure my cooperation?" His voice was an unrecognizable snarl.

"I'm going to ignore that question," the witch said. "I don't feel Terrin's presence at all, Michael. Would she have left on her own?"

"She's only six!" Michael lurched to his feet. "Where would she have gone?" His voice rose with every word. "She's only six, Espen! And your house was supposed to be safe!"

"Michael." Alban's voice wasn't loud enough to puncture his fury.

He had been routed from his familiar house to a place he could no longer call home. He had lost his daughter, only to regain her again, and come close to losing his life. He'd spent a night as Terrin's prisoner, found his mother, and had been forced to confront pieces of his past that he had tried so hard to forget. He wanted to lash out at something--anything--but he could not allow his temper to get the best of him now.

He needed to be clearheaded for this. No matter how bad things became, he had certain...rules to follow now, as a Council member, and he had to remember their guidelines.

Michael took a deep breath and closed his eyes. He took another deep breath and felt the helpless fury start to trickle away. Oh, worry was still there, and he doubted the sick churning in his stomach would go away until Enapay was safe, but he could think now.

For the moment, at least.

When he opened his eyes, Alban stood in front of him, biting his bottom lip like a hesitating child. Espen stood on Michael's other side. The glow of her healing magic glittered from her fingertips; no doubt prevention if he would lose his temper and do something unthinkable

"I don't think Espen had anything to do with Enapay's disappearance," the vampire said. He had not risen from his chair. In fact, at the moment, he looked worse than Alban, who still stood near Michael, struggling not to let exhaustion weaken his limbs.

Michael sank down on the edge of Alban's bed when he realized his legs would not support his weight. "I know." But it was difficult not to lash out at something. Or someone. Should he have stayed with her instead of following Espen to his mother? Should he have checked on her one last time?

Tears coursed down his cheeks, but he made no move to wipe them away. What could he do? How would Sarah react if he returned home without Enapay? He took another deep breath. "You said...you said you didn't feel Terrin's presence at all."

"That's right," Espen said. "And I still don't."

"Could you be wrong?" Michael asked the question without any thought as to how Espen would react. As soon as he realized he had spoken it, he flinched, waiting for the explosion.

But Espen merely smiled. "If the taint of his presence was light enough, then perhaps I would not feel it," she said. "Do you feel it when a mosquito lands on your arm? When a fly lands in your hair?"

She had a point. Michael could give her that much, at least.

"What about...you said you couldn't feel Zaira either." For some reason, their previous conversation rose up in his mind. Had she seen something? Learned something about Enapay that forced her to act? "Perhaps she took Enapay away to save her life," Michael whispered, desperate to cling to something positive.

"Perhaps she did," she said, her voice almost syrupy smooth. She stepped inside the room and gently helped Alban back to his bed.

Michael glanced at her suspiciously, but her hands were not glowing with the telltale Healer power, and she seemed sincere. And her voice did help soothe his anger. He took another deep breath.

"Why else would they leave?"

A movement near the door caught his attention and he glanced up in time to see a half-familiar figure shadowed in the doorway.

Espen's face tightened. "Teluride? What are you doing out of bed?" To Michael, she said, "Teluride is heir to Leysan's throne. Terrin drugged him."

Teluride ventured a small smile, even though he looked exhausted. "I lost my memory," he said by way of explanation. "Should I know you?"

"No, we've never met." There was something surreal about Teluride's admission, almost as if he had seen something like it before. He had wanted to lose his memory, more than once, but he'd never had the luxury of forgetfulness. "My name is Michael. I'm..." He glanced at Espen. "I'm Skade's son." The declaration felt strange in his mouth, almost as if it did not belong to him at all.

Teluride didn't realize the import of that statement, and Michael didn't expect him to. "Zaira came to me before she left." He leaned against the door, more for support than anything else.

"She did?" Espen's voice had lost all edge of comfort. "And what did she say?"

Teluride pushed a lock of dark hair out of his eyes. "She said she was sorry, but this was the only way. She seemed very upset, but she was determined that she had to leave."

"Did she give you any other information at all?" Michael asked. "She...took my daughter with her, you see. And...Enapay's only...she's only six years old."

Teluride shook his head. "She didn't mention your daughter. I'm sorry."

"What did she mention?" Espen asked. "Did she give you any details at all?"

"No." Teluride was visibly weakened now. He swayed where he stood, but no one made a move to help him. "She just said..."

Michael stood, crossed the room, and took his arm. Teluride leaned on him gratefully. "She said this was the only way."

"To vanish? To leave the only safe place in the Seven Kingdoms and not tell anyone where she plans to go?" Espen took Teluride's other arm. Together, they helped him to the bed. "Did she say anything else?"

Teluride shook his head, momentarily winded. "Just that it was better this way, and she had to go."

"Nothing else?"

"No," Teluride whispered. "I'm sorry, Espen. I thought she would know best, but when I awoke, I wondered if *I* had dreamed of her leaving. So I checked her room, but she wasn't there. And she said she Dreamed something horrible that wouldn't come true if she ran away."

"Damn," Espen said forcefully. "I wish she had confided in me before she took it upon herself to leave. Michael, I might need your help to find them. We're short a Dreamer at the moment..." her voice trailed away. "No we aren't. Nicodemus is healed; all I have to do is ask him to find both girls and I'm sure he will do it."

Michael rubbed his eyes. "I don't understand how he can be alive," he said. "He died in my mother's arms. I saw it. I was there."

"Well, he's not dead now," Espen said. "I healed his wounds, but none of them seemed life-threatening,"

"Terrin stabbed him in the *chest*!" Michael stared at her. "How could that not be life..." He froze as a horrible thought came to mind. "Espen..." The thought was almost too horrible to utter. "Espen...are you *positive* that was Nicodemus Zaira found?"

In the stark silence that reigned after the implications of that question arose in everyone's minds, Michael clearly heard a door ease closed down the hall.

Down the hall.

He had mentally counted off the rooms in his mind, before. Teluride's was first, then Zaira's. Enapay's came next, then Michael's. Across from Michael's room was an empty room, and then the one they all crowded inside. He had not reached the second to last bedroom, and the last...

Michael erupted from the bed. "Mother!"

Chapter 27

"I'm glad you're not dead, Nicodemus," Enapay said gravely as soon as Nicodemus opened his eyes.

Zaira watched him carefully. "I think everyone thought you were dead."

He licked his lips. "*I* thought I was dead." He focused his eyes on the trees surrounding them. "Where are we?"

"I think," Zaira hesitated and glanced at Enapay. "I think Espen's wards are keeping us out."

"A Healer cannot turn away a supplicant," Nicodemus whispered and struggled to his knees. "I can see her wards. We're very near." He reached out his hand, but blurring vision made it impossible to see the shifting lines of Espen's wards. "You dragged me here?" He felt both leaves and dirt embedded in his hair.

"We couldn't carry you," Enapay said, as if speaking to a little child. "Zaira thought we should get as close as possible to Espen's house." She sounded as if she quoted that last part.

"We tried to carry you, but you were too heavy," Zaira explained. "Time is running out. Someone will die if we don't get past Espen's wards soon." Her eyes unfocused and stared past Nicodemus. "Someone could already be dead."

Nicodemus had not Dreamed at all of this future, but he had Cathan's conversation with Terrin to back up her Dreams. "I know. I...heard Cathan and Terrin talking. Cathan's supposed to kill Skade...to kill My Queen." The words felt strange in his mouth, as if they no longer belonged. "Cathan wanted to kill Teluride while wearing your face, Zaira. But I think Terrin talked him out of it."

An indescribable expression passed across Zaira's face; a mixture of relief, guilt, and fear. "Then it wasn't me. What I saw...really wasn't me."

For a moment, Nicodemus did not understand, and then he realized what she must have thought, seeing Teluride--or Skade, he did not know which--murdered by someone who looked exactly like her. His flesh chilled at the very thought.

"No, it wasn't you."

Zaira closed her eyes. "Good." When she opened them, her gaze was bright again, and full of purpose. "How will we get past Espen's wards?"

"I believe to do that you must be in need of a Healer," a new--and dreaded voice--said from behind them.

Enapay gasped. Zaira stared in horror. Nicodemus recognized Terrin's voice immediately and remembered what he had said to Cathan. "I'm sorry," he whispered to Zaira and Enapay. "I knew he was coming. But I couldn't move fast enough."

He was determined, even weak as he was, to protect the two girls at all cost--even at the cost of his life. He managed to turn, keeping Zaira and Enapay behind him.

"What an interesting tableau," Terrin said. "An escaped prisoner, my erstwhile Dreamer, and a little brat. I'm surprised to see you, Nicodemus. I thought you were dead again."

"Evidently not," Nicodemus rasped.

Terrin's lips curled into a thin smile. "Not yet, at least. I'll remedy that situation as soon as you're in a place with no reflective surfaces so you won't be able to escape this time."

"There were no mirrors in your tower," Nicodemus pointed out, and wondered why Cathan hadn't bothered to tell him about the crystal. Was he keeping it as a last resort?

"Don't mock me," Terrin growled. "You might have survived once, but no one has survived my spell a second time, Nicodemus. Remember that."

What would happen if Terrin struck him with the spell again? He had healed remarkably fast from the wounds he had nearly died from, but the healing had taken the remnants of what strength he had possessed. Nicodemus didn't remember much of the past few days, but he thought the pain of Terrin's spell had come very close to killing him.

"You need someone to carry a message for you," he finally said. "Let Zaira and Enapay go. Espen won't turn them away."

"I distinctly heard Zaira say she couldn't get past Espen's wards," Terrin snapped. "And messengers have no basis in my plan. No, Nicodemus, it's best if I gather up as many hostages as possible. After all, once Cathan does his duty, Espen's wards will be in shambles."

Nicodemus didn't remember hearing anything about the breaking of Espen's wards, but he had not heard the entire conversation. "What do you mean?" A split second after he asked that question, he realized he should have acted more surprised to hear Cathan's name.

Terrin frowned at Zaira. "Have you been sharing your Dreams again?"

"You know I must," Zaira said, her voice and bearing oddly unafraid.

"I discovered a few things after I spoke to Cathan," Terrin said. "Just an interesting tidbit of information that might interest all of you."

"What is it?" Enapay asked crossly.

Nicodemus almost smiled at the expression that passed across Terrin's face.

"If someone is killed while in a Healer's care, the death negates the Healer's power. Your precious Espen will be powerless against me."

If he spoke true, that meant everyone still inside Espen's cottage would be helpless against Terrin's wrath. And since the loss of Espen's protections would move the course of events in his favor, Nicodemus saw no reason why he would lie. He glanced at Zaira and Enapay, who stared up at him in horror. He wracked his brain for ideas, but he came up with nothing.

He had no power to fight Terrin; his talents lay in other areas. Like portal-making, and Dreaming. Absolutely nothing that would help him now.

Or...perhaps...they *were* only ten feet from the stream, after all. And Espen's wards flowed through the stream, close enough to touch. If he could reach the stream and form a portal, he might be able to send Zaira and Enapay to the dubious safety of Espen's cottage.

Before he could act, Enapay broke away and ran. Terrin shouted, but the little girl dodged a blast of fire that Espen *had* to have felt, and vanished into the trees.

Nicodemus launched himself at Terrin. "Run!" he yelled to Zaira, but could not check to see if she obeyed. He hit Terrin awkwardly, unable to put much leverage behind his attempt, but even his weak try was enough to push Terrin off-balance.

They fell in a tangle of limbs and curses. A moment later, Terrin pushed him off and scrambled up, but Zaira had already vanished into the trees. Nicodemus rolled away and stretched out one hand to touch the stream, ignoring Terrin's curses behind him. The portal formed on pure adrenaline, slicing through Espen's wards like a razor-sharp blade. Nicodemus screamed as Espen's wards backlashed into him, pounding what was left of his strength into dust.

Inside Espen's cottage, the crystal around Cathan's neck shattered. Nicodemus bit through his lip and forced his last shred of strength through the portal.

Terrin's hand closed over his shoulder. A dagger pricked the back of his neck, and the weight of Terrin's knee dug into his back. "Release your portal," Terrin growled.

Nicodemus gasped in a shallow breath. The portal was molten fire in his mind, stripping away all semblance of coherent thought much more effectively than Terrin's spell itself. He did not try to speak.

"Release it!" Terrin pulled him up and jerked him away from the stream, but the joining was not broken by the absence of touch. An arc of water followed Nicodemus across the forest floor, shining brightly even in sunlight.

Nicodemus could not release the portal now. That required strength, and he had none left to give.

But Terrin knew how to release the portal. He thrust down with his sword just as someone bypassed Espen's wards and pulled Nicodemus out of the way. Blind from the pain, he could do nothing but sag in his rescuer's grip.

Inexplicably, Terrin began to laugh. "You've killed *yourself*, my lady."

"No," Nicodemus whispered, struggling in her grasp. "No."

Skade's grip abruptly lessened. Nicodemus turned just in time to catch her, but he could not support her weight.

And the portal, their only means of escape, collapsed in a wash of water that knocked Nicodemus to his knees. He lowered Skade to the ground, ignoring Terrin for now. His Queen was all that mattered.

In sunlight, his Queen's skin was almost transparent, and her eyes sunken deep in shadow. She was not dead yet.

"Someone wearing your face walked into my room as bold as you please," Skade whispered, lifting one hand to touch the side of his face. "But I felt no sense of loyalty from him. And he tried to kill me."

"It was Cathan," Nicodemus whispered.

Terrin cursed behind him.

"Then I felt you..." Her voice dropped. "And I used your power to come here." Pale lips twitched in what could have been a smile. "I...I thought I had enough strength to save you, but I guess I don't."

"Get away from her," Terrin ordered.

Nicodemus ignored him. "My Queen...I can't let you die."

"I don't think you have much of a choice, Mirror," Skade whispered.

Nicodemus could *see* Terrin's spell eating away at her strength and her body, leaving nothing but an empty husk behind.

And if he could see the spell...if he could *see* it woven through her body like a mismatched rug...if he could see it, could he not also unweave it?

He touched the side of her face, greatly daring to be so familiar. "My Queen, I cannot let you die." He had no idea if she could guess at what he planned to do, but he hoped she understood the reason for his sacrifice.

Ever so gently, he lifted a piece of the glowing knot of Terrin's spell. It seeped under his skin, immediately attacking his body as it had attacked hers. His fingers tingled with its passage, the tingle soon becoming a raging torrent that stripped every nerve in his arm raw.

"What are you doing?" Terrin grabbed the collar of his shirt and pulled him back. Nicodemus broke contact with Skade's skin, but not before another layer of Terrin's spell transferred itself from her body to his. How much would he have to take from her for his Queen to live? Half? All of it? Did it matter? He pulled out of Terrin's grasp and grabbed Skade's hand.

Terrin sliced through his shirt with the blade of his sword. Nicodemus felt a hot ribbon of blood slide down his back, but he couldn't pay attention to it now. He had to save Skade's life first. Her life was all that mattered.

Terrin swung again and opened up Nicodemus' arm from shoulder to elbow. Despite the renewed pain, Nicodemus tightened his grip on Skade's hand and desperately pulled in the sticky threads of Terrin's spell.

He had done this once before, for Teluride, but this time hurt much worse than before. He gagged when Terrin's spell rose up to close his throat, and desperately tried to breathe.

Skade's grip tightened. "Nicodemus, what are you doing?"

She sounded stronger already, even though he had taken less than half of Terrin's spell from her body.

He closed his eyes as Terrin's sword sank into his side. "Saving your life, my Queen."

Their roles abruptly reversed. Skade wrenched her hand from his grasp and struggled to her feet. "Terrin, stop!"

"Why?" Terrin snarled. "I killed him once; I *will* do it again." He raised his sword for the killing blow.

Nicodemus closed his eyes. He had no strength left to fight. Blackness rushed to envelop him and he did not push it away.

He felt Skade drop to her knees beside him. "I will not let you kill him again," she said, her voice as strong as steel. Her hands touched his skin; explored his wounds. Nicodemus tasted blood in the back of his throat. He cracked open his eyes as Terrin thrust the sword towards his unprotected chest, and had to gasp when Skade grabbed the bare and bloody blade to stop it three inches above his heart.

For a moment they stood frozen: wizard and Queen, locked in a struggle of strength and will. Then a curious thing happened. Before Terrin could jerk the sword from Skade's grasp, the mingled blood on the blade began to glow.

And in that glow, through some miracle Nicodemus did not understand, the tendrils of Terrin's spell that still raged through Skade's body began to die.

Skade understood what was happening long before Terrin. *She* pulled it from Terrin's grasp and threw it behind her into the weeds. "Nicodemus is under my protection," she said, her voice just as strong as old. She smoothed down her skirt with her unwounded hand. Nicodemus could not tear his gaze away from her beauty.

"You..." Terrin's eyes narrowed. "That's impossible. You should be dead."

Skade smiled. "I should be. But I'm not." She raised back her head and gave him her best glare. "In fact, I feel quite restored."

"Impossible," Terrin snapped. "You're no Dreamer. I would have known."

Skade staunched the wound in Nicodemus' side. "You're right, I'm not." She spoke as if Terrin mattered little. "But something happened. I feel fine."

"You can still be killed," Terrin whispered, his voice laden with ice.

"So can you," a new voice said behind Terrin. Towards the stream.

Nicodemus' hold on consciousness loosened and spun out of control. He struggled to hold the blackness at bay, but he had no strength left to struggle.

As Terrin turned to face this new threat, Nicodemus drifted away.

Chapter 28

Both the vampire and Alban could run faster than any of the others, and when Michael cried his mother's name, they were already moving. Alban lagged behind, but the vampire reached Skade's room first. Eschewing any element of surprise, he threw the door open, just in time to see Skade vanish into a mirror and a man who looked exactly like Nicodemus spin around.

The fake Nicodemus held a dagger in one hand. He stared at the vampire for a long moment, then curled his lip. "You'll do as well as Skade, I suppose."

Before he could attack, Michael did, moving in with no weapons of his own. The fight was oddly silent until Michael pinned the fake Nicodemus against his mother's bed.

"Where is Enapay, Cathan?" Fury had robbed Michael's voice of all emotion. "Where is my daughter?"

"I don't know," Cathan growled. "I haven't seen the little brat, and I don't *want* to see her!"

When Espen stepped into the room, Cathan stopped struggling and stared up at her, still through Nicodemus' eyes.

"The ruse is up," she said, her voice tired. "Change back into your rightful shape, Cathan."

The change was subtle at first, but then unmistakable. The vampire didn't recognize the man Michael pinned to the bed, but he hadn't expected to. As a shapeshifter, Cathan could become anyone. And the vampire uneasily wondered if he had come across Cathan before and not realized it. After Terrin had taken away his name, he had seen a lot, but not enough to damn him. Not nearly enough.

"I can't hold prisoners here," Espen said, "but I imagine we can find room in Iomar's dungeons for him. What do you think, Michael?"

For the first time, Michael seemed to realize that Skade was not in the room. "What? Espen, where's my mother?" He ground Cathan's head into the bedsheets. "Where is my mother?"

Cathan spat out a scrap of lace. "Which would you prefer, your mother or your daughter?" he sneered, his face changing with every word. The woman he became: young, with short brown hair and a thin, pixie-like face, was no one the vampire had ever seen before.

Michael, on the other hand, reacted as if he had been stabbed. He jumped back with a startled yell, and Cathan lunged at him with another dagger.

This time, Alban reacted before the vampire could move. His brother grabbed a wooden chair and swung it in Cathan's path. Cathan collided with the chair and fell, hitting the back of his head on the edge of Skade's bedframe. The dagger slid across the floor and stopped at Espen's feet.

"I saw Skade escape through a portal," the vampire whispered in the sudden silence. "She can't have gone far."

"Right outside, I think," Espen said, touching the mirror Skade had used. "Someone tried to get in before, using a portal, but my wards stopped them. I wonder..."

The vampire heard the kitchen door crash open. Espen whirled 'round, then vanished completely from the room, evidently expecting an attack.

Michael nudged Cathan's motionless form with the toe of his boot. "Thank you, Alban." He knelt to tie Cathan's wrists and ankles together, using strips of cloth from Skade's sheets.

A moment later, a babble of excited voices drifted up the hall. Michael ran out of the room at the sound of Enapay's voice, but the vampire didn't want to leave their prisoner alone.

"I'll stay with him," Teluride said from behind him. "You two go on ahead."

With one last dubious glance at Cathan, the vampire followed Alban to the kitchen, where Zaira and Enapay were in the midst of a detailed explanation that seemed to involve Nicodemus alive again, Terrin, and Cathan plotting to kill Teluride. Enapay flew into Michael's arms as soon as she saw her father.

"Terrin's outside," Espen said. "I can feel him right outside my wards. I'm not sure, but I think your mother is there as well."

The vampire wondered why she didn't mention Nicodemus, but he kept his silence.

"I have to go to her," Michael said, giving Enapay one last hug. He stood.

"You know I can't come with you," Espen said.

Michael nodded. "I know." He hesitated, then turned to the vampire. "I want you and Alban to stay here."

Since the sun shone down over the forest, the vampire had no quarrel with staying behind, but he thought he should do something, at least. "I will watch you from the mirror and help if I can."

Michael nodded. "Thank you."

Zaira started to say something, then stiffened and closed her eyes. For a long moment, everyone in the room watched her face, waiting for her to speak.

"You'll want a mirror," she finally said. "A small one, like this." She held out her hands in a loose circle.

Espen rummaged in a drawer and came up with a small mirror. Michael took it and tucked it into his back pocket. He hesitated, and the vampire knew he wanted to ask the question in everyone's minds, but he finally shook his head.

"I'm not going to ask. I'll be back as soon as I can." He said this with much more certainty than the vampire could have mustered.

"You'll come back," the vampire said, his eyes suddenly blinded by tears.

Michael nodded. "I'll come back."

And then he was gone, vanished into the sunlight where the vampire could not go, to fight a fight that was not truly his own; to rescue his mother and, perhaps, Nicodemus.

The vampire blinked away his tears and turned to Zaira. "He'll come back?"

She nodded, but her face was troubled. "He'll come back."

Only later did he realize he had not asked *who* would not return to Espen's care.

Chapter 29

They were not difficult to find. Michael followed the raised voices first, and then he saw his mother kneeling--kneeling!--over Nicodemus' body. Terrin stood a few feet away, weaponless. Michael spotted his sword lying in the grass at the edge of the trees and claimed it for his own.

When a new voice drifted out of the trees, Michael took advantage of that distraction to move up beside his mother. She glanced up at him, her gaze full of life now, with no sign of Terrin's spell. Michael remembered what the vampire had said and wondered if Nicodemus had known the cure as well. Or had they shared blood by accident?

If Nicodemus died, he might never know.

Terrin saw him approach and scowled. "Have you come to protect her? Or do you want to die with her, Michael?" His lip curled. "Where is your daughter?"

"She's safe," Michael said, refusing to rise to the bait. Behind Terrin, an unfamiliar woman emerged from the forest. She had short-cropped black hair and wore all blacks and grays, but her clothes were travel-stained and dusty. While Terrin's attention was on Michael, she held up something Michael did not recognize, but Skade obviously did.

The Queen of Iomar smiled and nodded her head. Confused, Terrin turned, and his scowl deepened further to see the woman behind him. "So, you both escaped. I should have brought you here and saved you the journey."

"Perhaps you should have," the woman said. "But if I hadn't left of my own accord, I wouldn't have found willing witnesses to the murders you committed in Glinyeu."

"Help me up," Skade murmured to Michael, who complied. "I wondered how he managed to become so powerful so quickly. What did he do, Kyne?" She directed this last question at the dark haired stranger.

Kyne. Michael wracked his memory for that name, but nothing came to light. Still, it seemed he should know her, even then.

"Sister to the Queen of Severin," Skade whispered, as if she'd read his mind.

"Witnesses?" Terrin laughed. "Witness to what? I did nothing wrong."

"You murdered over a hundred people for your own gain, Terrin." Kyne shook her head. "Did you think you would get away with it? Did you think you would never be punished for your crimes? If you add in the murder of your brother and his Council besides..."

"I did not kill my brother," Terrin snarled. "Teluride did. He was found with the dagger in his hand."

But especially now, that argument seemed all the more flimsy. And Terrin seemed to know it. He stared at Kyne for a full minute, then swung back to glare at Skade and Michael. His lips moved, but Michael could not hear what he said.

Skade held up her hand. Terrin started for her, but Michael beat him back with Terrin's own sword. Kyne threw the object she held in her hand--

an object that turned out to be a single red bead that shone in the sunlight as it flew over Terrin's head.

Skade caught the bead and it burst into flame. She smiled a terrible smile. "So be it."

At the last second, Michael realized what Terrin planned to do. At the last second, he snatched the mirror out of his pocket and held it up to hold Terrin's reflection as Terrin loosed his spell one final time.

The force knocked Michael to his knees. The mirror cracked.

And Terrin screamed, and kept screaming, until his spell devoured him.

You can find ALL our books up on our website at:

http://www.writers-exchange.com

All Jennifer's books:

http://www.writers-exchange.com/Jennifer-St-Clair/

all our fantasy novels:

http://www.writers-exchange.com/category/genres/fantasy/

About the Author

Jennifer St. Clair grew up in Southern Ohio and spent most of her childhood in the woods around her home. She wrote her first novel when she was thirteen, and hasn't stopped since. She lives with her ball python, Fester, and two cats, Ash and Rowan.

In her spare time, she crochets, makes cloth dolls, collects antiques, books, and vintage clothing, and takes digital photographs with varying degrees of success.

Her *Beth-Hill series* is set in the area in America that contains many supernatural creatures: Wild Hunt, Vampires, Dragons, Faery and more.

It is part of the Universe that her *Jacob Lane Series, Karen Montgomery Series* and vampire trilogy, *The Shadow Series* are set in.

Follow all her books on her author page:

http://www.writers-exchange.com/Jennifer-St-Clair/

If you want to read more about other books by this author, they are listed on the following pages...

A Beth-Hill Novel (Stand Alone Novels)

Are creatures of the night and all manner of extramundane beings drawn to certain locations in the natural world? In the Midwestern village of Beth-Hill located in southern Ohio, the population is made up of its fair share of common citizens...and much more than its share of supernatural residents. Take a walk on the wild side in this unusual place where imagination meets reality.

Blood of Innocents

Ten years ago, Orien, crown prince of the Seleighe, was captured by his mortal enemies, locked in a dungeon and turned into a vampire. Six years into Orien's sentence, the Healer's brother Cullen disobeyed his mistress's orders to kill him and turned him into a vampire instead, thus sealing both their fates for all eternity.

Now both Orien and Cullen are set free. But a secret only Cullen knows lies locked inside his mind, threatening to drive him mad before he can uncover the identity of a traitor--the very elf who betrayed Orien and left them both to die in darkness.

Publisher: http://www.writers-exchange.com/blood-of-innocents/

Full Moon

Werewolves change into wolves when the moon is full. But Edward's curse only allows him to be *human* when the moon is full.

Alone and despairing, Edward hides himself away from the world. He's scraped out a meager existence for himself for almost a century in the forest he's grown to love and call home. But in the depths of a terrible winter, he stumbles across clues from the life his mother left behind in Faerie. The truth may give him the answers he needs about the source of his birthright... and the curse that holds him captive.

Publisher: http://www.writers-exchange.com/full-moon/

A Beth-Hill Novel: Jacob Lane Series

Are creatures of the night and all manner of extramundane beings drawn to certain locations in the natural world? In the Midwestern village of Beth-Hill located in southern Ohio, the population is made up of its fair share of common citizens...and much more than its share of supernatural residents.

Jacob Lane is a ten-year-old girl who's spent her life unaware of her magical heritage. After being sent to Darkbrook, a school of magic, supernatural mysteries seem to spring to life all around her and her new friends.

Book 1: The Tenth Ghost

After Jacob Lane's parents mysteriously vanish, she's sent to Darkbrook, the only school of magic in the United States. While there, she and her new friends stumble upon a series of mysterious deaths in the nine ghosts that haunt the halls of Darkbrook. These ghosts were students who died at the school over the past hundred years. Will Jacob become the tenth ghost, or can she stop a witch's reign of terror?

Publisher: http://www.writers-exchange.com/the-tenth-ghost/

Book 2: The Ninth Guest

When Jacob's friend Ophelia's family decides to open up their castle for guests, amateur paranormal sleuth Jacob Lane is invited to join in on the fun. "Spend the night in a vampire's castle and live to tell the tale!" is supposed to be a fundraiser to help Ophelia's family pay the bills. Heating a castle costs quite a bit, after all. But, after the truth of an old secret is uncovered, what began as an innocent business venture soon turns deadly when vampire hunters get involved.

For years, the vampire hunters have had only one goal: To destroy all vampires. With the help of a new friend, Jacob and Ophelia must work together to save the entire VonBriggle family from extinction.

Publisher: http://www.writers-exchange.com/the-ninth-guest/

Book 3: The Eighth Room

For two hundred years, the Selkies have kept themselves separate from those who live on land. But now the Selkies need allies or they'll be crushed by their ancient enemies, the Finfolk.

Jacob and Ophelia, students at the only school of magic in the United States, uncover a mystery that dates back to Darkbrook's beginnings. While helping clean out old storage rooms for classroom expansion, they find something that might save the Selkies from extinction. With the help of the youngest member of the Wild Hunt who are no longer so wild or terrifying, they must foil the Finfolk who desire the Selkie's destruction...or die trying.

Publisher: http://www.writers-exchange.com/the-eighth-room/

Book 4: The Seventh Secret

After a picture of Niklas, the dragons' liaison to the only school of magic in the United States, shows up in too many newspapers to count, Darkbrook is forced to go on the defensive. The secret of Darkbrook's existence has been discovered. But there are more than dragonhunters in the forest, and, as Jacob Lane, supernatural sleuth and student at Darkbrook, learns how to use her newly discovered talent of healing, she helps to right an old wrong and must battle a teenaged wizard intent on proving--once and for all--that magic is real.

Publisher: http://www.writers-exchange.com/the-seventh-secret/

Book 5: The Sixth Stone

Jacob Lane, supernatural sleuth, and Danny, her werewolf friend, stumble across an alternate world where the Wild Hunt was never bound, and Darkbrook, the school of magic they attend, was abandoned a hundred years ago.

But when the Hounds of the Hunt wish to surrender, the two students are swept up in a whirlwind of heartbreak, betrayal, and the discovery of a lost treasure.

Publisher: http://www.writers-exchange.com/the-sixth-stone/

A Beth-Hill Novella: Karen Montgomery Series

Are creatures of the night and all manner of extramundane beings drawn to certain locations in the natural world? In the Midwestern village of Beth-Hill located in southern Ohio, the population is made up of its fair share of common citizens...and much more than its share of supernatural residents. Take a walk on the wild side in this unusual place where imagination meets reality.

Karen Montgomery was an ordinary woman until she stumbled into the extraordinary... A bargain with elves worth its weight in gold. A plague of sinister ladybugs. Rogue vampire hunters, including one who tries to turn over a new leaf--with disastrous consequences. A ghostly huntsmen of the Wild Hunt wishing for redemption. Karen's life will never be the same again.

Book 1: Budget Cuts

Karen Montgomery is used to taking care of the unpleasant jobs no one else wants to deal with. When a shortage of funds forces her to fire fifteen employees from the library, she isn't happy, but the nasty task has to be done and she is, after all, the boss. But Karen finds finishing her task impossible when she can't seem to track down Ivy Bedinghaus, a night clerk she's never actually met. Once she finally does confront Ivy, she's thrust into a centuries-old conflict that makes her previous troubles radically pale in comparison.

Publisher: http://www.writers-exchange.com/budget-cuts/

Book 2: The Secret of Redemption

Karen Montgomery, librarian, finds herself embroiled in another otherworldly adventure...

A member of the Wild Hunt--ghostly myths that aren't so ghostly (or myth-like) anymore--needs help in reconciling who he once was in life and who he is now.

A little girl has gone missing. And the one most likely responsible for her disappearance is the one Karen must prove innocent.

Publisher: http://www.writers-exchange.com/the-secret-of-redemption/

Book 3: Ladybug, Ladybug

An innocent attempt to rid the library of a plague of ladybugs turns sinister when a rogue vampire hunter gets the contract for pest control.

Ivy Bedinghaus, who works for Karen as a night clerk--along with all the vampires in Beth-Hill--are in danger, and their only hope for survival is with the help of Karen, a member of the Wild Hunt, and Russell Moore, a reformed vampire hunter.

Publisher: http://www.writers-exchange.com/ladybug-ladybug/

Book 4: Detour

One wrong turn sends Karen down a road that shouldn't exist, to the site of an old accident and an even older mystery. With reformed vampire hunter Russell Moore's help, Karen finds the key to the mystery. But Russ keeps his own secrets...some of which are deadly.

When old friends from Russ' past come to call, Karen realizes his secrets might just mean his doom. After a terrible incident three years ago, before Karen met him, Russ wants only to live the rest of his life quietly in Beth-Hill. But his secret might not allow him the new lease on life Russ longs for.

Publisher: http://www.writers-exchange.com/detour/

Companion Story: Russ' Story: Capture

Long before Russell Moore ever met supernatural sleuth Karen Montgomery or set foot in Beth-Hill, he was a vampire hunter, possibly the best vampire hunter of all. He brought down whole nests of vampires, caring little about the consequences of his actions. Anyone who lived with or helped the vampires became enemies to be slaughtered.

So what kind of an idiot would capture a ruthless vampire hunter without a conscience and try to reform him?

Ethan Walker was that idiot. Wanting to protect his family, Ethan set out to prove to Russ that vampires weren't all evil, soulless creatures. If Russ would allow himself to witness their lives, see their humanity, surely he and other vampire hunters like him would let them live in peace. *Surely?*

Publisher: http://www.writers-exchange.com/capture/

Secrets When in Shadow Lie

Twelve years ago, Ryan Grey was cursed by a witch to hide a secret. He's lived with the curse of being unable to die permanently, and, over the years he's slowly losing the memory of his past until almost nothing remains.

But now, after a chance meeting with an elf named Zipporah, he discovers the key to unlocking the secret and breaking the curse once and for all...if he can survive the breaking.

Publisher: http://www.writers-exchange.com/secrets-when-in-shadow-lie/

The Dead Who Do Not Sleep

Will Spark only wants a good night's sleep after a night of drinking. Instead, two thugs bang on his door, demanding answers to questions he can't understand. And then they killed him...

Publisher: http://www.writers-exchange.com/the-dead-who-do-not-sleep/

A Beth-Hill Novel: The Abby Duncan Series

Are creatures of the night and all manner of extramundane beings drawn to certain locations in the natural world? In the Midwestern village of Beth-Hill located in southern Ohio, the population is made up of its fair share of common citizens...and much more than its share of supernatural residents. Take a walk on the wild side in this unusual place where imagination meets reality.

Situated in Beth-Hill, where imagination meets reality, is The Rose Emporium, owned by elderly and not-a-little-odd Rose Duncan. The large Victorian house smackdab in the middle of nowhere is a cross between a pawn shop and an antique store that caters to supernatural creatures needing to barter. Rose's twenty-something niece, Abby Duncan, discovers that the world isn't made up of just run-of-the-mill, ordinary humans but an entire spectrum of unusual beings. With her preconceptions about what's normal and what's not turned upside-down, Abby is in for a whole lot of startling truths, mysteries-- about herself and the people and places around her--and danger.

Novella 1: By Any Other Name

Woodturner Abby Duncan decides to sell her spindles at a local Renaissance Festival with only some success. After all, no one really spins their own yarn anymore, do they? While there, she discovers that one of her newfound friends is not what he appears--and his secret is about to get him killed!

Publisher: http://www.writers-exchange.com/by-any-other-name/

Book 2: The Uncrowned Queen

Abby Duncan's elderly Aunt Rose has always been a bit odd. And now she's off on a mysterious trip, leaving Abby behind to run the Rose Emporium, an unusual sort of antique shop. Such an extraordinary store would have been a perfect place for Seth and the others, her friends from the Renaissance Festival, to take a break from traveling between Faires. But when tragedy strikes and Abby and the others discover the true nature of the Rose Emporium, they'll have to travel into Faerie itself before their tightknit group is whole again.

Abby doesn't know much about her family history, but she's about to find out the truth...whether she likes it or not.

Publisher: http://www.writers-exchange.com/the-uncrowned-queen/

Book 3: Coming Soon!

A Beth-Hill Novel: The Shadows Trilogy

Are creatures of the night and all manner of extramundane beings drawn to certain locations in the natural world? In the Midwestern village of Beth-Hill located in southern Ohio, the population is made up of its fair share of common citizens...and much more than its share of supernatural residents. Take a walk on the wild side in this unusual place where imagination meets reality.

A Dreamer dreams the future when the past is not yet laid to rest. Ten years ago, a plague swept across the Seven Kingdoms. Ten years ago, the Queen of Iomar's son was exiled and named the author of the magical plague. Now, in the present, Terrin works to complete his ultimate goal: Control of the Seven Kingdoms using his son's power to supplement his own. But his attempt at dominion meets resistance and the fate of the world rests in the unlikely hands of an exiled prince, a Dreamer, and a vampire...

Book 1: The Prince of Shadows

When Alban's father Terrin appeared at the castle door with a vampire in tow and apologies on his lips, Alban fell under his spell just like everyone else and welcomed him home. But Terrin didn't return to live quietly in his brother's kingdom. He had other plans and, with Alban's untrained powers at his disposal, he begins his ruthless plan to destroy the Seven Kingdoms and rule them all, beginning with his brother's death.

Terrin engineers events to cast the blame on his nephew, Teluride, intending to see the boy executed for his father's murder. But there are those who would thwart Terrin in his mad plan for power, and Alban forms an unlikely alliance with Skade, the reclusive Queen of Iomar, and Terrin's slave, a young vampire with no memory of his name or origins. Although the future looks grim, Alban and the vampire attempt to stop Terrin...and they almost succeed.

A darker history lies at the heart of Terrin's treachery, and only Skade knows the true reason why Terrin would murder his own brother and attempt to destroy both Alban and the vampire to achieve his goals. The Ghost who resides in Skade's mirror--her servant and thrall--holds one of the keys to Terrin's madness. Unfortunately, more than one person wishes for the past to remain the past and the future to hold no shadows of what might have been...

Publisher: http://www.writers-exchange.com/the-prince-of-shadows/

Book 2: Lost In Shadows

Events set in motion ten years ago come to a head as Skade, the reclusive Queen of Iomar, and Nicodemus, who is imprisoned by Skade, struggle to free Alban and the vampire from Terrin's grasp. Old secrets come to light when Skade's exiled son is forced to face his past--or die trying to redeem himself once and for all. Can the crimes of the past truly be forgiven? Only time will tell...and time is running out.

Publisher: http://www.writers-exchange.com/lost-in-shadows/

Book 3: Bound In Shadows

With his power crushed, brother to the king and father to Alban, Terrin is forced to take drastic measures to regain his sons after they are freed and harness the power they possess. But he has an ally inside the healer's house where they are recovering who works to further his plans. The Queen of Iomar, Skade's son, courts redemption to try to save his mother's life, and the vampire who no longer remembers his own name dreams a dream that might save them all...or damn them if success is thwarted.

Publisher: http://www.writers-exchange.com/bound-in-shadows/

A Beth-Hill Novel: Wild Hunt Series

Are creatures of the night and all manner of extramundane beings drawn to certain locations in the natural world? In the Midwestern village of Beth-Hill located in southern Ohio, the population is made up of its fair share of common citizens...and much more than its share of supernatural residents. Take a walk on the wild side in this unusual place where imagination meets reality.

The Wild Hunt roamed the forest outside of Beth-Hill until the Council bound them for a hundred years. Nevertheless, a century of existence has made an indelible mark not easily forgotten for these ghostly myths that are no longer so ghostly or myth-like...

Book 1: Heart's Desire

The Wild Hunt roamed the forest outside of Beth-Hill until the Council bound them for a hundred years--a lifetime for a human but only a passing thought to one such as Gabriel, Master of the Wild Hunt. As the Council's binding draws to a close, old enemies reappear to ensure that the Wild Hunt is bound once more--to a creature much worse than the Council has been.

Publisher: http://www.writers-exchange.com/hearts-desire/

Book 2: Fire and Water

As a young vampire, Erialas Morgan brought his mother back to life with a spell that shouldn't exist, shouldn't have worked...perhaps shouldn't have been performed at all. Desperation and love are his only excuses for doing the unthinkable.

There are others who wish to use that same spell for their own gain--and to destroy the Wild Hunt once and for all. Caught in the middle of a war between the Morgan clan of vampires and their human kin, Erialas turns to the Hunt for help. But even Gabriel, the Master of the Wild Hunt, may not be able to stop the tide of death and destruction once it turns.

Publisher: http://www.writers-exchange.com/fire-and-water/

Book 3: The Lost

Almost sixty years ago, Darkbrook, the only school of magic in the United States, opened its doors to students of decidedly different natures, sending out letters of invitation to the elves, the dragons, and the vampires. The three who responded to the invitation banded together despite their differences but vanished only weeks later along with an entire classroom full of students and their teacher after a field trip gone horribly wrong.

The Wild Hunt has healed and the Hounds have grown closer together, keeping Darkbrook's forest safe and secure for those who live there. Malachi, one of the eldest members of the Wild Hunt, has adapted to Josiah's spell to help him see, but when a demon boy trapped in the body of a human body for sixty years inside the school disrupts the newfound calm, the Hunt--and those they protect--are thrust into a struggle that should have ended long ago when a vampire, an elf, and a dragon vanished into the Mists.

Publisher: http://www.writers-exchange.com/the-lost/

Book 4: A Glint of Silver

Jericho is a vampire who wants is to live away from the Richmond household of vampires led by his ruthless father Connor. When Jericho tries to escape, Connor punishes him and leaves him to die. Tristan is determined to be the one to bring Jericho back, but he can't see him suffer for wanting a normal life. As long as Connor lives, Jericho will never be safe or free. As long as Connor *lives*...

Publisher: http://www.writers-exchange.com/a-glint-of-silver/

Book 5: All That Glitters

As a member of the cruel Morgan Household of vampires, twelve-year-old Arthur Morgan has been abused all his life.

Maya, a water fairy, shows him just how horrible and twisted the household he's grown up is. With her help, and the unexpected help of an adult vampire, Arthur attempts to escape.

Can he become something more than what his father has decreed?

Publisher: http://www.writers-exchange.com/all-that-glitters/

The Chelsea Chronicles

Normally a quiet, serene place, Chelsea Kingdom seems like the perfect location for a centuries' old vampire to blend in and live a normal life, even escape hunters and an angry mob. Unfortunately, his timing couldn't be worse...

Book 1: So You Want to be a Vampire

Chelsea Kingdom is usually a pretty quiet place but recent murders--committed by a vampire--upset the calm. Newcomer to town, Vlad Dhalgren wants only to blend in and live a normal life. He quickly learns that isn't possible, given that other vampires have been hiding in the shadows around the castle--in plain sight--for years.

Despite her lineage, Anna Everett, the crown princess of the Kingdom of Chelsea, isn't a wizard like her father, which means she will never be Queen. She has only one friend, Valerian Moreton--Val--who has secrets he's never shared that could get him *and* Anna killed...

Publisher: http://www.writers-exchange.com/so-you-want-to-be-a-vampire/

Book 2: Transformation

As Anna, crown princess of Chelsea, adjusts to life as a vampire after recent events, Vlad plans for a future he has no real hope to seeing come to pass due to injuries sustained while attempting to save Anna's life. But, as life goes on for Anna and her friend Valerian "Val" Moreton, it changes for others--some of whom are not quite what they seem...

Publisher: http://www.writers-exchange.com/transformation/

You can find ALL our books up on our website at:

http://www.writers-exchange.com

All Jennifer's books:

http://www.writers-exchange.com/Jennifer-St-Clair/

all our fantasy novels:

http://www.writers-exchange.com/category/genres/fantasy/